ALEXANDER McCALL SMITH

At the Villa of Reduced Circumstances

Alexander McCall Smith is the author of the huge international phenomenon, The No. 1 Ladies' Detective Agency series, and The Sunday Philosophy Club series. He is a professor of medical law at Edinburgh University. He was born in what is now known as Zimbabwe, and he was a law professor at the University of Botswana. He lives in Scotland.

BOOKS BY ALEXANDER McCALL SMITH

At the Villa of
Reduced Circumstances

ALEXANDER McCALL SMITH

At the Villa
of Reduced
Circumstances

Illustrations by
Iain McIntosh

ANCHOR BOOKS
A Division of Random House, Inc.
New York

This is for Marvin and Margaret Sloman

FIRST ANCHOR BOOKS EDITION, JANUARY 2005

Copyright © 2003 by Alexander McCall Smith
Illustrations copyright © 2003 Iain McIntosh

Cataloging-in-Publication Data for
At the Villa of Reduced Circumstances is on file
at the Library of Congress.

ISBN 1-4000-9509-3

Author photograph © Chris Watts

www.anchorbooks.com

Printed in the United States of America
20 19 18 17 16 15 14 13 12

Contents

ON BEING LIGHT BLUE

PROFESSOR DR MORITZ-MARIA VON IGELFELD's birthday fell on the first of May. He would not always have remembered it had the anniversary not occurred on May Day itself; as a small boy he had been convinced that the newspaper photographs of parades in Red Square, those intimidating displays of missiles, and the grim-faced line-up of Politburo officials, all had something to do with the fact that he was turning six or seven, or whatever birthday it was. Such is the complete confidence of childhood that we are each of us at the centre of the world – a conviction out of which not all of us grow, and those who do grow out of it sometimes do so only with some difficulty. And this is so very understandable; as Auden remarked, how fascinating is that class of which I am the only member.

Nobody observed von Igelfeld's birthday now. It was true that he was not entirely alone in the world – there were cousins in Graz, but they were on the Austrian side of the family and the two branches of von Igelfelds, separated by both distance and nationality, had drifted apart. There was an elderly aunt in Munich, and another aged female relative in Baden-Baden, but they had both forgotten more or less everything and it had been many years since they had sent him a birthday card. If he had married, as he had firmly intended to do, then he undoubtedly would now have been surrounded by a loving wife and children, who would have made much of his birthday; but his resolution to propose to a charming dentist, Dr Lisbetta von Brautheim, had been thwarted by his colleague, Professor Dr Detlev Amadeus Unterholzer. That was a humiliation which von Igelfeld had found hard to bear. That Unterholzer of all people – a man whose work on the orthography of Romance languages was barely mentioned these days; a man whose idea of art was coloured reproductions of views of the Rhine; a man whose nose was so large and obtrusive, vulgar even, the sort of nose one saw on head-waiters – that Unterholzer should succeed in marrying Dr von Brautheim when he himself had planned to do so, was quite unacceptable. But the fact remained that there was nothing one could do about it; Unterholzer's birthday never went unmarked. Indeed, there were always cakes at coffee time in the Institute on Unterholzer's birthday, made by Frau Dr Unterholzer herself; as Unterholzer pointed out, she might be a dentist but she had a sweet tooth nonetheless and made wonderful, quite wonderful cakes and pastries. And then there were the cards prominently displayed on his desk, not only from Unterholzer's wife but from the receptionist and dental nurse in her practice. What did they care about Unterholzer? von Igelfeld asked himself. They could hardly *like* him, and so they must have sent the cards out of deference to their employer. That was not only wrong – a form of exploitation indeed – but it was also sickeningly sentimental, and if that was what happened on birthdays then he was best off without one, or at least best off without one to which anybody paid any attention.

On the first of May in question, von Igelfeld was in the Institute coffee room before anybody else. They normally all arrived at the same time, with a degree of punctuality which would have been admired by Immanuel Kant himself, but on that particular morning von Igelfeld would treat himself to an extra ten minutes' break. Besides, if he arrived early, he could sit in the chair which Unterholzer normally contrived to occupy, and which von Igelfeld believed was more comfortable than any other in the room. As the best chair in the room it should by rights have gone to him, as he was, after all, the senior scholar, but these things were difficult to articulate in a formal way and he had been obliged to tolerate Unterholzer's occupation of the chair. It would have been different, of course, if Professor Dr Dr Florianus Prinzel had taken that chair; von Igelfeld would have been delighted to let Prinzel have it, as he undoubtedly deserved it. He and Prinzel had been friends together at Heidelberg, in their youth, and he still thought of Prinzel as the scholar-athlete, the noble youth, deserving of every consideration. Yes, there was little he would not have done for Prinzel, and it was a matter of secret regret to von Igelfeld that he had never actually been called upon to save Prinzel's life. That would have secured Prinzel's undying admiration and indebtedness, which von Igelfeld would have worn lightly. 'It was nothing,' he imagined himself saying. 'One's own personal safety is irrelevant in such circumstances. Believe me, I know that you would have done the same for me.'

In fact, the only time that Prinzel had been in danger von Igelfeld had either been responsible for creating the peril in the first place, or Prinzel had been able to handle the situation quite well without any assistance from him. In their student days in Heidelberg, von Igelfeld had unwisely persuaded Prinzel to engage in a duel with a shady member of some student *Korps*, and this, of course, had been disastrous. The very tip of Prinzel's nose had been sliced off by his opponent's sword, and although it had been sewn back on in hospital, the doctor, who had been slightly drunk, had sewn it on upside down. Prinzel had never said anything about this, being too gentlemanly to complain about such an affair (no true gentleman ever notices it if the tip of his nose is sliced off), and indeed it had occurred to von Igelfeld that he had not even been aware of what had happened. But it remained a reminder of an unfortunate incident, and von Igelfeld preferred not to think about it.

That was one incident. The other occasion on which Prinzel had been in danger was when von Igelfeld had accompanied him and his wife to Venice, at a time when the city was threatened by an insidious corruption. The corruption turned out not to be cholera, as so graphically portrayed by Thomas Mann, but radio-activity in the water, and Prinzel had become mildly radioactive as a result of swimming off the Lido. Again von Igelfeld was unable to come to the rescue, and Prinzel, quite calmly, had taken the situation in hand and returned to Germany for iodine treatment at the University of Mainz. There he had been decontaminated and pronounced safe, or as safe as one could be after ingesting small quantities of strontium-90.

Thoughts of radioactivity, however, were far from von Igelfeld's mind as he enjoyed his first cup of coffee in the Institute coffee room and glanced at the headlines in the *Frankfurter Allgemeine Zeitung*. There was nothing of note, of course. Industri-alists were sounding off about interest rates, as they always did, and there was a picture of an earnest finance minister pointing a finger at a chart. The chart could have been upside down, like Prinzel's nose, for all that von Igelfeld cared; matters of this sort left him unmoved. It was the job of politicians and bankers to run the economy and he could not understand why they often failed to do so in a competent way. It was, he assumed, something to do with their general venality and with the fact that quite the wrong type went into politics and finance. But it seemed as if there would never be any change in that, and so they would have to put up with these insolent people and with their persistent mismanagement. Far more interesting was the front-page item about a row which was developing over the appointment of a new director to a museum in Wiesbaden.

The new director, a man of modern tastes, had thrown out the old cases of fossils and rocks, and had replaced them with installations by contemporary artists. This had the effect of confusing those people who came to the museum hoping to see items of interest and found only empty galleries with a small pile of wooden boxes in a corner or a heap of old clothing, artistically arranged under a skylight and labelled: *The Garments of Identity*. These visitors peered into the wooden boxes, hoping to see fossils or rocks within, and found that they were empty, and that the boxes themselves were the exhibit. And as for the piles of clothing, what was the difference between them and the museum cloakroom, where people hung their overcoats? Were both not *Garments of Identity*, or would it be confusing to label the cloakroom *Garments of Identity*? Would people know that it was a cloakroom, or would they search in vain for a room labelled *Cloakroom*? Von Igelfeld frowned. This sort of thing was becoming far too common in Germany, and he had every sympathy with the friends of the fossils and rocks who were attempting to secure the new director's resignation. This was far more interesting than news of interest rates, and far more significant, too, von Igelfeld thought. What if the levers of power at universities were to fall into similar hands to the hands of this new director? Would he himself be considered a fossil or a rock, and thrown out, to be replaced, perhaps, by a wooden box? How would Romance philology survive in a world that honoured the works of Joseph Beuys and the like?

It was while von Igelfeld was thinking of these dire possibilities that he heard the door of the coffee room open. He looked up, to see his colleagues entering, deep in what appeared to be animated conversation. There was sudden silence when they saw von Igelfeld.

'Good morning,' said von Igelfeld, laying the newspaper to one side. 'It seems that I am here first today.'

For a moment nothing was said. Then the Librarian cleared his throat and spoke. 'That would appear to be so, Herr von Igelfeld. And seeing you here solves the mystery which I was discussing with Professor Dr Prinzel outside, in the corridor. "Where is Professor Dr von Igelfeld?" I asked. And Professor Dr Prinzel said that he did not know. Well, now we all know. You are here, in the coffee room, sitting in . . . ' He tailed off, and moved quickly to the table where the coffee pot and cups stood in readiness.

They served themselves coffee in silence, and then came to join von Igelfeld around his table.

'How is your aunt?' von Igelfeld asked the Librarian. 'This spring weather will be cheering her up, no doubt.' The health of his demanding aunt was the Librarian's main topic of conversation, and it was rare for anybody to raise it, as they had all heard everything there was to be said about this aunt.

'That is very kind of you to ask,' said the Librarian. 'Very thoughtful. I shall tell my aunt that you asked after her. That will make her very happy. So few people care about people like her these days. It's good that at least somebody remembers.' He paused, throwing a sideways glance at Unterholzer and Prinzel. 'She will be very pleased indeed, I can assure you. And she does need some cheering up, now that they have changed her medicine and the new one takes some getting used to. It's Dutch, you know. I wasn't aware that the Dutch made medicines at all, but this one is said to be very good. The only problem is that it irritates her stomach and that makes her querulous at times. Not that she is always like that; it seems to be at its worst about twenty minutes after taking the pill in question. They come in peculiar yellow and white capsules, which are actually quite difficult to swallow. The last ones were white, and had the manufacturers' initials stamped into every capsule. Quite remarkable . . . '

It was Unterholzer who interrupted him. 'So,' he said. 'So this is a special day, is it not?'

Prinzel glanced nervously at Unterholzer. He had been hoping that he would not make an issue of the chair, but it seemed that he might. Really, this was most unwise. Everybody knew that von Igelfeld could be difficult, and Unterholzer really had no *legal* claim on that chair. He might have a moral claim, as people undoubtedly did develop moral claims to chairs, but this was quite different from a claim which could be defended in the face of a direct challenge. It would be far better to pass over the whole incident and for Unterholzer simply to arrive slightly early the following morning and secure the chair for himself. He could surely count on their moral support in any such manoeuvre.

'Today, you see,' Unterholzer went on, 'today is special because it is the birthday of our dear colleague, Professor Dr von Igelfeld.'

'My!' exclaimed the Librarian. 'The same month as my aunt! Hers is on the twelfth. What a coincidence!'

'May Day,' said Prinzel. 'A distress signal at sea, but for you quite the opposite!'

They all laughed at the witticism. Prinzel was so amusing and could be counted upon to bring a welcome note of levity, particularly to a potentially difficult situation.

Von Igelfeld smiled. 'It is very kind of you to remember, Herr Unterholzer,' he said. 'I had not intended to celebrate it.'

Unterholzer looked thoughtful. 'I suppose not,' he said. 'A birthday can't be much fun when one has to celebrate it all by oneself. There's no point, really.'

Von Igelfeld stared at him. Unterholzer often took the opportunity to condescend to him, if he thought he could get away with it, and this was quite intolerable. If anybody deserved to be pitied, it was Unterholzer himself, with his wretched, out-of-date book on Portuguese subjunctives, and that nose. Who was he even to hint that von Igelfeld's life might be incomplete in some way? It defied belief; it really did. He would tell Zimmermann himself about it, and Zimmermann, he knew, would laugh. He always laughed when Unterholzer's name was mentioned, even before anything else was said.

Prinzel intervened rapidly. 'I remember, Moritz-Maria, how we used to celebrate our birthdays, back in Heidelberg, when we were students. Do you remember when we went to that inn where the innkeeper gave us free steins of beer when he heard it was your birthday. He always used to call you the Baron! "Free beer for the Baron's birthday," he said. Those were his very words, were they not?'

Unterholzer listened closely, but with increasing impatience. This Heidelberg story had irritated him, and he was beginning to regret his act of generosity – supererogatory in the provocative circumstances – in drawing attention to von Igelfeld's birthday. He had not anticipated that Prinzel would launch into this embarrassing tribute to von Igelfeld. 'So why did he call Professor Dr von Igelfeld a baron, when he isn't one?' he asked. 'Why would anyone do that?'

Prinzel smiled. 'Because some people, even if they aren't barons in the *technical* sense have – how shall I put it?; this really is a bit embarrassing – some of the *qualities* that one normally associates with that position in life. That is why, for example, that my friend Charles von Klain is often addressed as *Capitano* by the proprietors of Italian restaurants. He has the appropriate bearing. He has no military rank, but he could have. Do you see what I mean?'

Unterholzer shook his head. 'I do not see why people should be called Baron or Count, or even *Capitano* for that matter, when they are not entitled to these titles.'

'It is not an important thing,' said von Igelfeld. 'It is really nothing.'

'But it is!' said the Librarian. 'These things are important. One of the doctors who visits my aunt's nursing home is a Polish count. Of course he doesn't use the title, but do you know, one of the other patients there, a charming lady from Berlin, could spot it. She said to my aunt: "That Dr Wlavoski is an aristocrat. I can tell." And do you know, when they asked the Director of the nursing home, he confirmed it! He explained that the Wlavoskis had been an important family of landowners in the East and they had been dispossessed – first by our own authorities when they invaded – and that was most unfortunate and regrettable – and then again by the Russians when they came in. They were a very scientifically distinguished family and they all became physicians or astronomers or the like, but the fact that they had been counts somehow shone through.'

They all looked at the Librarian. The conversation was

intensely embarrassing to von Igelfeld. The von Igelfelds were certainly not from that extensive and ubiquitous class of people, the 'vegetable nobles' (for whom *von* was nothing more than an address). Of course he could be addressed as Baron by only the very smallest extension of the rules of entitlement; after all, his father's cousin had been the Freiherr von Igelfeld, the title having been granted to the family by the Emperor Francis II, and on his mother's side there were barons and baronesses aplenty, but this was not something that people like him liked to discuss.

'Perhaps we should change the subject,' said Prinzel, who could sense Unterholzer's hostility. The problem there was that Unterholzer would have liked to have been mistaken for a baron, but never could be. It was out of the question. And it was not just a question of physical appearance – which alone would have precluded it – it was something to do with manner. Unterholzer was just too . . . too clumsy to pass for anything but what he was, which was a man of very obscure origins from some dim and undistinguished town in a potato-growing area somewhere.

'Yes,' said Unterholzer. 'A good idea. We are, after all, meant to be serious people. Talk about barons and all such nonsense is suitable only for those silly magazines that you see at the railway station. Such silliness. It's surprising that it survives. So let us talk about your birthday, Herr von Igelfeld! How are you going to celebrate it?'

'I am not proposing to do anything in particular,' said von Igelfeld. 'I shall possibly go out for dinner somewhere. I don't know. I have not thought about it.'

'A birthday is a good time to review the past year,' said Prinzel. 'I always think over what I've done. It's useful to do that.'

'Or indeed to review one's entire life,' suggested Unterholzer.

'You might think with some satisfaction of all your achievements, Herr von Igelfeld.' This remark was quite sincere. In spite of his envy, Unterholzer admired von Igelfeld, and would have liked to have been more like him. He would have loved to have written *Portuguese Irregular Verbs* himself and to have enjoyed von Igelfeld's undoubted distinction. But of course he had not, and, in moments of real honesty, he acknowledged that he never would.

'Yes,' said Prinzel. 'You have done so much. You could even write your autobiography. And when you wrote it, the final chapter would be: Things Still Left to be Done. That would allow it to end on a positive note.'

'Such as?' interjected Unterholzer. 'What has Professor Dr von Igelfeld still to do?'

'I have no idea,' said Prinzel. 'He has done so much. We had better ask him.' He turned to von Igelfeld, who was taking a sip of his coffee. 'What would you really like to do, Herr von Igelfeld?'

Von Igelfeld put down his coffee cup and thought for a moment. They were right. He had done so much; he had been to so many conferences; he had delivered so many lectures; he had written so many learned papers. And yet, there were things undone, that he would like to do. He would like, for example, to have gone to Cambridge, as Zimmermann had done only a few years before. They had given Zimmermann a lodge for a year when he had been a visiting professor and von Igelfeld had visited him there. The day of his visit had been a perfect summer day, and after taking tea on the lawns of the lodge they had driven out to Grantchester in Zimmermann's car and had drunk more tea possibly under the very chestnut trees which Rupert Brooke had referred to in his poem. And von Igelfeld had felt so content, and so pleased with the scholarly atmosphere, that he had decided that one day he too would like to follow in Zimmermann's footsteps and visit this curious English city with its colleges and its lanes and its feeling of gentleness.

'I should like to go to Cambridge,' he announced. 'And indeed one day I shall go there.'

Unterholzer listened with interest. If von Igelfeld were to go to Cambridge for an appreciable length of time, then he might be able to get his office for the duration of his time away. It was a far better office than his own, and if he simply moved in while von Igelfeld was away nobody would wish to make a fuss. After all, what was the point of having empty space? He could give his own office over to one of the research assistants, who currently had to share with another. It was the logical thing to do. And so he decided, there and then, to contact his friend at the German Scholarly Exchange Programme and see whether he could fix an invitation for von Igelfeld to go to Cambridge for a period of six months or so. A year would be acceptable, of course, but one would not want to be too greedy.

'I hope your wish comes true,' said Unterholzer, raising his coffee cup in a toast to von Igelfeld. 'To Cambridge!'

They all raised their coffee cups and von Igelfeld smiled modestly. 'It would be most agreeable,' he said. 'But perhaps it will never happen.'

'My dear Professor von Igelfeld!' said the Master, as he received von Igelfeld in the drawing room of the Lodge. 'You really are most welcome to Cambridge. I take it that the journey from Regensburg went well. Of course it will have.'

Von Igelfeld smiled, and bowed slightly to the Master. He wondered why the Master should have made the Panglossian

assumption that the journey went well. In his experience, journeys usually did not go well. They were full of humiliations and assaults on the senses; smells that one would rather not smell; people one would rather not meet; and incidents that one would rather had not happened. Perhaps the Master never went anywhere, or only went as far as London. If that were the case, then he might fondly imagine that travel was a comfortable experience.

'No,' said von Igelfeld. 'It was not a good journey. In fact, quite the opposite.'

The Master looked aghast. 'My dear Professor von Igelfeld! What on earth went wrong? What on earth happened?'

'My train kept stopping and starting,' said von Igelfeld. 'And then my travelling companions were far from ideal.'

'Ah!' said the Master. 'We cannot always choose the company we are obliged to keep. Even in heaven, I suspect, we shall have to put up with some people whom we might not have chosen to spend eternity with, were we given the chance. Hah!'

Von Igelfeld stared at the Master. Was this a serious remark, to which he was expected to respond? The English were very difficult to read; half the things they said were not meant to be taken seriously, but it was impossible, if you were German, to detect which half this was. It may be that the Master was making a serious observation about the nature of the afterlife, or it may be that he thought that the whole idea of heaven was absurd. If it were the former, then von Igelfeld might be expected to respond with some suitable observation of his own, whereas if it were the latter he might be expected to smile, or even to laugh.

'The afterlife must surely be as Dante described it,' said von Igelfeld, after a short silence. 'And one's position in the circle will determine the company one keeps.'

The Master's eyes sparkled. 'Or the other way round, surely. The company one keeps will determine where one goes later on. Bad company; bad fate.'

'That is if one is easily influenced,' said von Igelfeld. 'A good man may keep bad company and remain good. I have seen that happen.'

'Where?' said the Master.

'At school,' said von Igelfeld. 'At my Gymnasium there was a boy called Müller, who was very kind. He was always giving presents to the younger boys and putting his arm around them. He cared for them deeply. He was in a class in which most of the other boys were very low, bad types. Müller used to put his arm around these boys too. He never changed his ways. His goodness survived the bad company.'

The Master listened to this story with some interest. 'Do people read Freud these days in Germany?' he asked.

Von Igelfeld was rather taken aback by this remark. What had Freud to do with Müller? Again there was this difficult English obliqueness. Perhaps he would become accustomed to it after a few months, but for the moment it was very disconcerting. In Germany people said what they meant; they had the virtue of being literal, and that meant that everything was much clearer. This was evidently not the case in Cambridge. 'I believe that he has his following,' said von Igelfeld. 'There are always people who are prepared to find the base motive in human action. Professor Freud is a godsend to them.'

The Master smiled. 'Of course, you are right to censure me,' he said. 'We live in an age of such corrosive cynicism, do we not?'

Von Igelfeld raised a hand in protest. 'But I have not censured you! I would never dream of censuring you! You are my host!' He was appalled at the misunderstanding. What had he said that had caused the Master to conclude that he was censuring him? Was it something to do with Freud? Freudians could be very sensitive, and it was possible that the Master was a Freudian. In which case, perhaps his remark had been rather like telling a religious person that his religious views were absurd.

'I meant no offence,' said von Igelfeld. 'I had no idea that you were so loyal to Vienna.'

The Master gave a start. 'Vienna? I know nothing about Vienna.'

'I was speaking metaphorically,' said von Igelfeld hastily. 'Vienna. Rome. These are places that stand for something beyond the place itself.'

'You are referring to Wittgenstein, I take it,' said the Master. 'There used to be some of the older dons who remembered him. A most unusual figure, you know. He used to like going to the cinemas in Cambridge, where he would eat buttered toast. Very strange behaviour, but acceptable in a man of that ability.'

Von Igelfeld smiled. 'I have never eaten toast in a cinema,' he said.

'Nor I,' said the Master, somewhat wistfully. 'There is so much in this life that I haven't done. So much. And when I think of the years, and how they slip past. *Eheu! Eheu, fugaces!*'

The Master looked up at von Igelfeld, at this tall visitor, and, extracting a handkerchief from his trouser pocket, he suddenly began to cry.

'Please excuse me,' he said, between sobs. 'It's not easy being the Master of a Cambridge college. People think it is, but it really isn't. It's hard, damnably hard! And I get no thanks for it, none at all. All I get is criticism and opposition, and moans and complaints from the College Fellows. Their rooms are too cold. The college wine cellars are not what they used to be. Somebody has removed the latest *Times Literary Supplement* and so on. All day. Every day. Oh, I don't know. Please excuse me. I know it doesn't help to cry, but I just can't help it. If you knew what it was like, you'd cry too. They say such beastly things to me. Beastly. Behind my back and sometimes to my face. Right to my face. I bet they didn't do that to Wittgenstein when he was here. I bet they didn't. They just pick on me. That's all they do.'

Von Igelfeld leaned forward and put an arm round the Master's shoulders. Just like Müller, he reflected.

Von Igelfeld was shown to his rooms by the Porter, a gaunt man who walked with a curious, halting gait up the winding stone stairway that led to von Igelfeld's door.

'A very good set of rooms, this is,' said the Porter. 'We reserve these rooms for the Master's personal guests and for distinguished visitors, like yourself, sir. You get a very fine view of the Court – probably the best view there is – and a passable view of the College Meadows.'

He unlocked a stout oak door on which von Igelfeld noticed that a painted name plate bearing his name had already been fixed. This was a pleasant touch, and he made a mental note to make sure that they made a similar gesture in future to visitors to the Institute. Or at least they would do it for some of their visitors; some they wished to discourage – some of Unterholzer's guests, for example – and it would be unwise to affix their names to anything.

The Porter showed von Igelfeld round the rooms. 'You have a small kitchen here, sir, but I expect that you'll want to eat in Hall with the other Fellows. The College keeps a good table, you know, and the Fellows like to take advantage of that. That's why we have so many fat academic gentlemen around the place, if you'll forgive the observation. Take Dr Hall out there, just for an example. You see him crossing the Court? He likes his food, does our Dr Hall. Always first in for lunch and always last out. Second helpings every time, the Steward tells me.'

Von Igelfeld moved to the window and peered out over the Court. A corpulent man with slicked-down dark hair, parted in the middle, was walking slowly along a path.

'That is Dr Hall?' he asked.

'The very same,' said the Porter. 'He's a mathematician, and I believe that he is a very famous one. Cambridge is well-known for its mathematicians. Professor Hawking, for example, who wrote that book, you know the one that everybody says they've read but haven't, he's a Fellow of that College over there, with the spire. You can just see it. There's him and there are plenty more like him.'

Von Igelfeld stared out of the window. He knew of *A Brief History of Time*, although he had certainly not read it. It had brought great fame to its author, there was no doubt about that, but did it really deserve it? *Portuguese Irregular Verbs* was probably of equal importance, but very few people had read it; that is, very few people outside the circles of Romance philology and there were only about . . . He thought for a moment. There were only about two hundred people throughout the world who were interested in Romance philology, and that meant that *Portuguese Irregular Verbs* was known to no more than that. His reflection went further: one could place all the readers of *Portuguese Irregular Verbs* in the Court below and still only a small part of it would be occupied. Whereas if one were to try to assemble in one place all the purchasers of Professor Hawking's book it would be like those great crowds in Mecca or on the banks of the Ganges during a religious festival. This was unquestionably unjust, and merely demonstrated, in his view, that the modern world was seriously lacking in important respects.

'I'm afraid these rooms lack a bathroom,' said the Porter, moving away from the window. 'That's the problem with these old buildings. They were built in the days before modern plumbing and it has been very difficult, indeed impossible, to make the necessary changes.'

Von Igelfeld was aghast. 'But if there is no bathroom, where am I to wash in the morning?'

'Oh, there is a bathroom,' said the Porter quickly. 'There's a shared bathroom on the landing. You share with Professor Waterfield. His rooms are on the other side of the landing from yours. There's a bathroom in the middle for both of you to use.'

Von Igelfeld frowned. 'But what if Professor Waterfield is in the bathroom when I need to use it? What then?'

'Well,' said the Porter, 'that can happen. I suppose you'll have to wait until he's finished. Then you can use it when he goes out. That's the way these things are normally done . . . ' adding, almost under his breath, 'in this country at least.'

Von Igelfeld pursed his lips. He was not accustomed to discussing such matters with porters. In Germany the whole issue of bathrooms would be handled by somebody with responsibilities for such matters; it would never have been appropriate for a professor, and especially one in a full chair, to have to talk about an issue of this sort. The situation was clearly intolerable, and the only thing to do would be to arrange with this Professor Waterfield, whoever he was, that he should refrain from using the bathroom during those hours that von Igelfeld might need it. He could use it to his heart's content at other times, but the bathroom would otherwise be exclusively available to von Igelfeld. That, he thought, was the best solution, and he would make the suggestion to this Professor Waterfield when they met.

The Porter in the meantime had extracted a key from his chain and handed this to von Igelfeld. 'I hope that you have a happy stay,' he said brightly. 'We are an unusual College, by and large, and it helps to have visitors.'

Von Igelfeld stared at the Porter. This was a very irregular remark, which would never have been made by a German porter. German porters acted as porters. They opened things and closed them. That was what they did. It seemed that in England things were rather different, and it was not surprising, then, that it was such a confused society. And here he was at the intellectual heart of this strange country, where porters commented on the girth of scholars, where bathrooms were shared by perfect strangers, and where masters of colleges, after making opaque remarks about Freud and Wittgenstein suddenly burst into tears. It would clearly require all one's wits to deal with such a society, and von Igelfeld was glad that he was a man of the world. It would be hopeless for somebody like Unterholzer, who would frankly lack the subtlety to cope with such circumstances; at least there was that to be thankful for – that it was he, and not Unterholzer, who had come here as Visiting Professor of Romance Philology.

That evening the Master invited von Igelfeld to join him and several of the Fellows for a glass of sherry before dinner. The invitation had come in a note pushed under von Igelfeld's door and was waiting for him on his return from a brief visit to the College Library. He had not spent much time in the Library, but he was able to establish even on the basis of the hour or so that he was there that there was an extensive collection of early Renaissance Spanish and Portuguese manuscripts in something called the Hughes-Davitt Bequest, and that these, as far as he could ascertain, had hardly been catalogued, let alone subjected to full scholarly analysis. The discovery had excited him, and already he was imagining the paper which would appear in the *Zeitschrift*: *Lusocripta Nova*: *an Untapped Collection of Renaissance Manuscripts in the Hughes-Davitt Bequest at Cambridge.* Readers would wonder – and well they might – why it had taken a German visiting scholar to discover what had been sitting under the noses of Cambridge philologists for so long, but that was an issue which von Igelfeld would tactfully refrain from discussing. People were used to the Germans discovering all sorts of things; most of Mycenaean civilisation had been unearthed by Schliemann and other German scholars in the nineteenth century, and the only reason why the British discovered the Minoans was because they more or less tripped up and fell into a hole, which happened to be filled with elaborate grave goods. There was not much credit in that, at least in von Igelfeld's view. The same could be said of Egyptology, although in that case one had to admit that there had been a minor British contribution, bumbling and amateurish though it was. Those eccentric English archaeologists who had stumbled into Egyptian tombs had more or less got what they deserved, in von Igelfeld's view, when they were struck down by mysterious curses (probably no more than long dormant microbes sealed into the pyramids). That would never have happened had it been German archaeology that made the discovery; the German professors would undoubtedly have sent their assistants in first, and it would have been they, not the professors themselves, who would have fallen victim. But it was no use thinking about English amateurism here in Cambridge, the very seat of the problem. If he did that, then everything would seem unsatisfactory, and that would be a profitless way of spending the next four months. So von Igelfeld decided to make no conscious comparisons with Germany, knowing what the inevitable conclusions would be.

He made his way to the Senior Common Room in good time, but when he arrived it seemed that everybody was already there, huddled around the Master, who was making a point with an animated gesture of his right hand.

'Ah, Professor von Igelfeld!' he said, detaching himself from his colleagues and striding across the room to meet his guest. 'So punctual! *Pünktlich* even. You'll find that we're a bit lax here. We allow ten minutes or so, sometimes fifteen.'

Von Igelfeld flushed. It was obvious that he had committed a solecism by arriving at the appointed time, but then, if they wanted him to arrive at six fifteen, why did they not ask him to do so?

'But I see that everybody else is here,' he said defensively, looking towards the group of Fellows. 'They must have arrived before six.'

The Master smiled. 'True, true,' he said. 'But of course most of them have little better to do. Anyway, please come and meet them. They are all so pleased that you took up the Visiting Professorship. The atmosphere is quite, how shall I put it? *electric* with anticipation.'

The Master took hold of von Igelfeld's elbow and steered him deftly across the room. There then followed introductions. Dr Marcus Poynton, Pure Mathematics; Dr Margaret Hodges, French Literature; Professor Hector MacQueen, Legal History (and history of cricket too); Mr Max Wilkinson, Applied Mathematics; and Dr C. A. D. Wood, Theoretical Physics.

'These are just a few of the Fellowship,' said the Master. 'You'll meet others over dinner. I thought I should invite a cross-section, so to speak.'

Von Igelfeld shook hands solemnly, and bowed slightly as each introduction was made. The Fellows smiled, and seemed welcoming, and while the Master went off to fetch a glass of sherry, von Igelfeld fell into easy conversation with the woman who had been introduced to him as Dr C. A. D. Wood.

'So you are a physicist,' said von Igelfeld. 'You are always up to something, you physicists. Looking for something or other. But once you find it, you just go off looking for something more microscopic. Your world is always getting smaller, is it not?'

She laughed. 'That's one way of putting it. In my case, I'm looking for Higgs's boson, a very elusive little particle that Professor Higgs says exists but which nobody has actually seen yet.'

'And will you find it?'

'If the mathematics are correct, it should be there,' she said.

'But can you not tell whether the mathematics are correct?' asked von Igelfeld. 'Can they not be checked for errors?'

Dr C. A. D. Wood took a sip of her sherry. 'It is not always that simple. There are disagreements in mathematics. There is not always one self-evident truth. Even here, in this College, there are mathematicians who . . . who . . . ' She paused. The Master had now returned with a glass of sherry for von Igelfeld.

'This is our own sherry, Professor von Igelfeld,' he said, handing him the glass. 'The Senior Tutor goes out to Jerez every couple of years and replenishes our stocks. He has a very fine palate.' He turned to Dr C. A. D. Wood. 'You have become acquainted with our guest, I see, Wood. You will see what I mean when I say that he is a very fine choice for the Visiting Professorship. Very fine.'

'Absolutely,' said Dr C. A. D. Wood.

'You were saying something about disagreements amongst mathematicians,' said von Igelfeld pleasantly. 'Please explain.'

At this remark, the Master turned sharply to Dr C. A. D. Wood and glared at her. 'I cannot imagine that Professor von Igelfeld is interested in such matters,' he hissed at her. 'For heaven's sake! He only arrived today, poor man!'

'I am most interested,' said von Igelfeld. 'You see, there are disagreements amongst philologists. Different views are taken. It seems that this is the case in all disciplines, even something as hard and fast as mathematics.'

'Hard and fast!' burst out Dr C. A. D. Wood. 'My dear Professor von Igelfeld, if you believe that matters are hard and fast in the world of mathematics, then you are sorely deluded.'

'I think Byzantine politics were harder and faster than mathematics,' sighed the Master. 'Or so it seems to me.'

'You know very little about it, Maestro,' said Dr C. A. D. Wood to the Master. 'You stick to whatever it is you do, old bean. Moral philosophy?'

Von Igelfeld felt uncomfortable. What had started as an innocent conversation – small talk really – had suddenly become charged with passion. It was difficult to make out what was going on – that problem with English obscurity again – and it was not clear to him why Dr C. A. D. Wood had addressed the Master as old bean. No doubt he would find out more about that, when Dr C. A. D. Wood had the opportunity to talk to him in private. In the meantime, he would have to concentrate on talking to the Master, who appeared to be becoming increasingly distressed. Dr C. A. D. Wood, he noticed, had drifted off to talk to Mr Wilkinson, who was looking steadfastly at his shoes while she addressed him.

'I am very comfortable in my rooms,' he said to the Master. 'I am very happy with that view of the Court. I shall be able to observe the comings and goings in the College, just by sitting at my window.'

'Oh,' said the Master. 'You will see everything then. The whole thing laid bare. Anaesthetised like a patient on the table, as Eliot so pithily said of the morning, or was it the evening, fussy pedant that he was. How awful. How frankly awful.'

'But why should it be awful?' asked von Igelfeld. 'What is awful about the life of the College?'

He realised immediately that he should not have asked the question, as the Master had seized his sleeve and was muttering, almost into his ear. 'They're the end, the utter end. All of them, or virtually all of them. That Dr C. A. D. Wood, for example, don't trust her for a moment. That's my only warning to you. Just don't trust her. And be very careful when they try to involve you in their scheming. Just be very careful.'

'I cannot imagine why they should wish to involve me in their scheming,' said von Igelfeld. 'I am merely a visitor.'

The Master gave a short chuckle. 'Visitors have a vote in this College,' he said. 'It's been in the statutes since 1465. Visiting Professors have a vote in the College Council. They'll want you to vote with them in whatever it is they're planning. And they're always planning something.'

'Who are *they*?' asked von Igelfeld. Was it the same *they* whom the Master had accused of persecuting him? Or was there more than one group of *theys*?

'You'll find out,' said the Master. 'Just you wait.'

Von Igelfeld looked into his sherry glass. There were those who said that the world of German academia was one of constant bickering. This, of course, was plainly not true, but if they could get a glimpse, just a glimpse, of Cambridge they would have something to talk about. And this was even before anybody had sat down for dinner. What would it be like once dinner was served or, and this was an even more alarming thing, over Stilton and coffee afterwards? And all the time he would have to be careful to navigate his way through these shoals of allusion and concealed meaning. Of course he would be able to do it – there could be no doubt about that – but it was not exactly what he had been looking forward to after a long and trying day. Oh to be back in Germany, with Prinzel and Frau Prinzel, sitting in their back garden drinking coffee and talking about the safe and utterly predictable affairs of the Institute. What a comfortable existence that had been, and to think that it would be four months, a full four months, before he could return to Regensburg and the proper, German way of doing things.

Shortly before they were due to go through for dinner, the Senior Common Room suddenly filled up with people, all wearing, as were von Igelfeld and the other Fellows, black academic gowns. At a signal from the Master, the entire company then processed through a narrow, panelled corridor and into the Great Hall which lay beyond. There, standing at their tables in the body of the Hall, were the undergraduates, all similarly gowned and respectfully waiting for the Master and Fellows to take their seats at the High Table.

The Hall was a magnificent room, dominated at the far end by an immense portrait of a man in black velvet pantaloons and with a bird of prey of some sort, a falcon perhaps, perched on his arm. Behind him, an idealised landscape was framed by coats of arms.

'Our founder,' explained the Master to von Igelfeld. 'William de Courcey. A splendid man who gave half of his fortune for the foundation of the College. He was later beheaded. So sad. I suspect that he was very charming company, when he still had his head. But then life in those days was so uncertain. One moment you were in favour and then the next you were *de trop*. His head, apparently, is buried in the Fellows' Garden. I have no idea where, but there is a particularly luxuriant wisteria bush which is said to be very old and I suspect that it might be under that. Possibly best not to know for certain.'

'You might erect a small plaque if you found the spot,' suggested von Igelfeld, as they took their seats at the High Table.

'Good heavens no!' said the Master, apparently shocked at the notion. 'Can you imagine how the Fellows would fight over the wording? Can't you just picture it? It's the last thing we'd do.'

Von Igelfeld was silent. It was impossible to discuss anything with the Master, he had decided; any attempt he made at conversation merely led to further diatribes against the Fellowship and, eventually, to tears. He would have to restrict himself to completely innocuous matters in any exchanges with the Master: the weather, perhaps; the English loved to talk about the weather, he had heard.

The Master, as was proper, sat at the head of the table, while von Igelfeld, as senior guest, occupied the place which had been reserved for such guests since the days of Charles II – the fourth seat down on the right, counting from the second seat after the Master's. On his left, again by immemorial custom, sat the Senior Tutor, and on his right, a small, bright-eyed man with an unruly mop of dark hair, Professor Prentice. On the other side of the table, directly opposite von Igelfeld, was Dr C. A. D. Wood, who was smiling broadly and who seemed to have quite got over their earlier conversation. She was flanked by Mr Wilkinson and by a person whom von Igelfeld realised he had seen before. But where? Had he met him in the Court, or had he seen him in the Library on his visit early that afternoon? He puzzled over this for a moment, and then the person in question moved his head slightly and von Igelfeld gained a better view of his features. It was the Porter.

Von Igelfeld drew in his breath. Was the Porter entitled to have dinner at High Table? Such a thing would never have happened in Germany. Herr Bomberg, who acted as concierge and general factotum at the Institute, always knocked three times before he came into the coffee room with a message and would never have dreamed of so much as sitting down, even if he were to be invited to do so. And yet here was the College Porter, breaking his bread roll on to his plate and engaging in earnest conversation with Dr C. A. D. Wood.

Von Igelfeld turned discreetly to the Senior Tutor. 'That person on Dr C. A. D. Wood's right,' he said. 'I have seen him somewhere before, I believe. Could you refresh my memory and tell me who he is?'

The Senior Tutor peered myopically over the table and then turned back to von Igelfeld. 'That's Dr Porter,' he said. 'A considerable historian. He works mainly on early Greek communities in the Levant. He wrote a wonderful book on the subject. Never read it myself, but I shall one day.'

'Dr Porter?' said von Igelfeld, aghast. It occurred to him that he had completely misread the situation and now, with a terrible pang of embarrassment, he remembered that he had tipped Dr Porter for showing him his rooms. The money had been courteously received, but, oh, what a solecism on his part.

'I thought he was *the* Porter,' said von Igelfeld weakly. 'He showed me to my rooms. I thought . . .'

'Oh, he does that from time to time,' said the Senior Tutor, laughing. 'It's his idea of a joke. He gets terribly bored with his Greek communities and he pretends to be the College Porter. He shows tourists round sometimes and gives the tips to the poorer undergraduates to spend on beer. He never pockets them himself.'

This explanation relieved von Igelfeld of his embarrassment, but embarrassment was now replaced by astonishment and a certain measure of alarm. The English were obviously every bit as eccentric as they were reputed to be, and this meant that further surprises were undoubtedly in store. He would have to be doubly vigilant if he were to avoid either humiliation or, what would be even worse, the commission of some resounding social mistake.

There was not a great deal of conversation over dinner itself. The Senior Tutor made the occasional remark, and von Igelfeld answered him, but this was hardly a conversational flow. Professor Prentice said a little bit more, but he confined himself to questions about German politicians, of whom von Igelfeld was largely ignorant. Then, shortly after the second course was served, he made a remark about the wine.

'Disgusting wine,' he said, sniffing ostentatiously at his glass. 'Ghastly stuff. You don't have to drink it if you don't want to, Professor von Igelfeld.'

The Senior Tutor pretended not to hear this remark, but it was clear to von Igelfeld that he had. He bit his lip, almost imperceptibly, and then raised his own glass.

'Carefully chosen wine, you know, von Igelfeld,' he said, mainly for the benefit of Professor Prentice. 'Not a wine that would be appreciated by the ignorant – quite the opposite, in fact. When I chose it – and I chose it personally, you know – I had in mind the slightly more *tutored* palate. Not a wine for undergraduates or *ouvriers*, you know. More for people who know what they're talking about, although, good heavens, there are precious few of those around these days.'

Von Igelfeld looked down at his glass, at a loss what to do.

'I am looking forward to drinking it,' he said at last, judging this to be the most tactful remark in the circumstances.

So the dinner continued, until at last the time came to return to the upstairs common room for coffee and port. There, with the Fellows and guests all seated in a circle, in ladder-backed chairs, the Junior Fellow circulated the port and conversation was resumed.

'Another visitor arrives tomorrow,' announced the Senior Tutor cheerfully. 'Our annual lecture on opera – an open lecture funded by the late Count Augusta, an immensely rich Italian who owned a helicopter factory. He studied here briefly as a young man and he left us a great deal of money, which he stipulated should be spent on opera matters. We've had some wonderful treats in the past.'

'Who is it this year, Senior Tutor?' asked one of the junior dons.

'Mr Matthew Gurewitsch,' announced the Senior Tutor. 'He is a well-known opera writer from New York and I am told that he is a very entertaining lecturer. He will be with us for one week exactly and then he goes on to interview Menotti. We are very lucky to have him.'

Von Igelfeld nodded approvingly. He knew little about opera, but was keen to learn more. It was possible that Mr Gurewitsch would talk about Wagner, or even Humperdinck, both of whom von Igelfeld approved of. But there were dangers; what if he chose to speak of Henze? For a moment he closed his eyes; to have to attend a lecture on Henze would be intolerable, the musical equivalent of attending a lecture on Beuys and his piles of clothes or his wooden boxes.

'And his subject?' asked another junior don.

'*Il Trovatore*,' said the Senior Tutor.

Von Igelfeld relaxed. He would attend the lecture, and attend with pleasure. Perhaps there would be indirect references to Wagner and to Humperdinck; one never knew what a lecturer was going to say until he started; or, should one say, until he finished.

Von Igelfeld spent the following morning in the Library. He made the acquaintance of the Librarian, who was delighted that somebody was prepared to work on the Hughes-Davitt Bequest.

'So few people seem to *care* about the Renaissance today,' said the Librarian. 'And yet, had it not happened, where would we be today?'

Von Igelfeld thought for a moment. Historical speculation of this sort was unprofitable, he thought. There was little point in thinking about that soldier who had prevented the spear from plunging into Alexander the Great and who had thus saved Western civilisation. But if he had not done so, and the Persians had conquered the Greeks, then ... He stopped himself. It was unthinkable the Institute itself might not have existed and yet it was quite possible, had history been rather different. Ultimately, we were all at the mercy of chance. All our schemes and enterprises were dependent on the merest whim of fate; as had been the outcome of that decisive naval battle when England defeated the Spanish Armada, but would not have done so had the wind come from a slightly different direction. In which case, the University of Cambridge itself would today be *La Universidad de Cambridge*, or *Pontecam*, to be precise.

At lunch time he returned to his rooms. He saw Dr Hall making his way purposefully towards the Refectory, and he remembered the uncharitable remarks of Dr Porter about stout dons. It was true, however, the dons at this College were very stout. Professor Waterfield, for example, whom he had met earlier that morning when they both arrived at the door of their shared bathroom at more or less the same time, was very stout indeed. There would certainly not be room for both of them in that bathroom should there be a struggle to see who would enter first.

There was, of course, no such struggle. Von Igelfeld politely asked Professor Waterfield whether he would care to return in twenty minutes, when the bathroom would again be vacant, and Professor Waterfield, although slightly surprised by von Igelfeld's suggestion, had mildly acquiesced.

'I should not wish to stand between you and cleanliness,' he remarked cheerfully as he returned to his room, and von Igelfeld, appreciating the quiet humour of this aside, responded: '*Mens sana in corpore abluto.*' Professor Waterfield did not appear to hear, or, if he did, chose not to say anything, which was a pity, thought von Igelfeld, as it was an aphorism that deserved a response. Perhaps he would have the opportunity to use it again when he next met his neighbour at the bathroom door; one never knew.

Now, beginning his ascent to his room, where he proposed to take his customary lunch-time siesta, he found himself face-to-face with a man whom he did not recognise from the previous evening's dinner. This person was carrying a suitcase and von Igelfeld, glancing down at it, saw the initials MG painted discreetly above the handle. This, he concluded, must be Mr Matthew Gurewitsch. He had noticed that the guest room on the floor below his, a distinctly inferior guest room, he had been led to believe, had been allocated to Mr Gurewitsch, and a small name card had been attached to the door in recognition of this arrangement. Feeling more confident of his surroundings, after he had introduced himself to Mr Gurewitsch, von Igelfeld showed him to his room, which was unlocked.

'A comfortable room,' said von Igelfeld, noting with pleasure that the furniture was distinctly more worn than his own. 'No bathroom, I'm afraid. But then these old buildings don't take too well to modern plumbing.'

'No bathroom!' exclaimed Mr Gurewitsch. 'Even the crypt on the set of *Aida* has hot and cold running water these days!'

'Well, that is opera,' said von Igelfeld. 'This is Cambridge. And it seems that there's no bathroom.'

'But what do I do?' asked Mr Gurewitsch.

'There's a bathroom over on the other side of the Court,' said von Igelfeld. 'It's attached to the Senior Common Room. I think that you will have to use that one.'

'You don't have one upstairs?' asked Matthew Gurewitsch hopefully.

Von Igelfeld was silent for a moment. If he told this new visitor about the bathroom that he shared with Professor Waterfield, then that would mean that there would be three people sharing, rather than two. Two was bad enough, of course – look what had happened that morning – but if there were three people using the one bathroom, that would be even worse. It did not matter that Mr Matthew Gurewitsch appeared to be an extremely agreeable man, it was purely a question of practicality. The bathroom issue was a problem which the College should face, and it was not up to visitors like von Igelfeld to have to shoulder the responsibility of everyone's bathroom needs. No, that would be to expect too much. He had no *locus standi* in bathroom matters in Cambridge and there was no moral obligation on his part to draw the attention of others to the existence of such bathroom facilities as there were.

At the same time, it was clear to von Igelfeld that he could not tell a lie. The motto of the von Igelfeld family was *Truth Always*, and he could not ignore this. It was true that he had deviated from it in that unfortunate encounter with Dr Max Augustus Hubertoffel, the psychoanalyst, but he had dealt with the moral sequelae of that lapse in as honourable a way as he could. But the incident had reminded him of the need for strict truthfulness. So his words would have to be chosen carefully, and here they were, forming themselves with no particular effort on his part: 'I do not have a bathroom in my rooms,' he said.

Although quite spontaneous, the words were well-chosen. It was indeed true that von Igelfeld did not have a bathroom in his rooms. There was a bathroom in the vicinity – on the landing to be precise – but this did not belong to von Igelfeld and therefore the precise terms of Matthew Gurewitsch's question did not require it to be disclosed. He felt sorry for Matthew Gurewitsch, and for the many others like him in Cambridge who presumably had no bathroom, and this prompted him to invite the new visitor to join him for coffee in the Senior Common Room.

'I could introduce you to some of the Fellows,' he said expansively. 'Dr C. A. D. Wood, Mr Wilkinson . . . ' He tailed off. Perhaps it was not a good idea. Poor Matthew Gurewitsch, no doubt exhausted after his journey, would hardly wish to be plunged into the unfathomable intrigues of mathematicians. 'Or we could talk just by ourselves,' he added. 'That might be better.'

Matthew Gurewitsch was happy to do either, and after he had found a place for his suitcase on a rather rickety table near the window, he and von Igelfeld made their way across the Court towards the Senior Common Room. Their conversation as they walked was easy, and von Igelfeld felt delighted that he should have made the acquaintance of this interesting man before people like Dr Hall, Dr C. A. D. Wood and the Senior Tutor could buttonhole him and effectively put him off Cambridge forever. Here was a man who really knew about his subject, and von Igelfeld revelled in the snippets of information – inside information – which studded his conversation. Had von Igelfeld seen the La Scala production of *Il Trovatore* last season? No? Well, did he know that the conductor had caused an uproar by playing the tenor's showstopper in the original key of C, rather than down half a step (*anglice*, tone) as is usually done so that tenors can more safely interpolate a climactic high note that Verdi never wrote? 'Of course,' Matthew Gurewitsch added, 'the inauthentic high note was omitted, too. That's what Italian musicologists call philology.'

Von Igelfeld expressed surprise, and remarked that in future one would have to watch that roles of counter-tenors were not taken down for the convenience of basses. Or even the Queen of the Night could be transcribed for *basso profondo*, thus removing all those troublesome moments for sopranos. Would that not make it easier? Matthew Gurewitsch had laughed.

'Everything is possible in opera these days,' he said. 'That is what I wish to talk about in my lecture. I want to look at what has happened to *Trovatore* recently. I want to issue a warning.'

'That is very wise,' said von Igelfeld. 'People must be warned.'

They entered the Senior Common Room, to find six or seven dons sitting in the various chairs which dotted the room. Dr C. A. D. Wood was present, and waved in a friendly fashion to von Igelfeld, and Dr Hall, who had decided against lunch in the refectory in favour of Stilton and biscuits in the Common Room, was sitting at a small table by himself, lost in quiet contentment.

Von Igelfeld took Matthew Gurewitsch over to Dr C. A. D. Wood and introduced them. She, in turn, made introductions to a rather mild-looking man who was sitting beside her, but who had stood up when the guests came to join them.

'This is Dr Plank,' she said.

Plank shook hands with von Igelfeld and then with Matthew Gurewitsch.

'I should warn you that you will not find Dr Plank's name in any College lists should you try to look for it,' remarked Dr C. A. D. Wood. 'And that is not because he is not a member of the College.'

This Delphic remark caused von Igelfeld to turn and look at Dr Plank, who had now sat down and had folded his hands over his stomach in a relaxed way. If this man were in disgrace of some sort, and had been excluded from the lists, then it did not appear to distress him. This was very strange, and there was something in Dr C. A. D. Wood's voice, an edge perhaps, which gave von Igelfeld the impression that she did not like Plank and was only sitting next to him on sufferance.

For a few moments, nothing was said. Matthew Gurewitsch glanced at Plank and then at von Igelfeld. Then he looked at Dr C. A. D. Wood. Dr C. A. D. Wood looked at Matthew Gurewitsch, and then at von Igelfeld. She did not look at Plank. Plank looked down at his shoes, and then across the room at Dr Hall, who looked back at him for a moment and then transferred his gaze to his Stilton.

Then Plank spoke. 'The reason why there's no Plank in the lists is not because there's no Plank – there is – but because Plank is not spelled Plank. That is why.'

Von Igelfeld looked puzzled. This was another English idiosyncrasy. How many ways were there of spelling Plank? Planc? Planque?

Plank appeared to be enjoying the guests' confusion. 'You may be aware,' he said, 'that there are various English surnames which are spelled and pronounced in quite different ways. One of the best-known examples is Featherstonehaugh, which is pronounced Fanshawe. Then there is Cholmondeley, which is simply pronounced Chumley, and of course anybody called Beauchamp is usually Beecham.'

Von Igelfeld nodded. 'I have noticed that,' he said. 'There was a Professor Chumley at a conference once and he pointed out that the spelling of his name was rather different. That would not happen in Germany.'

'No,' said Plank. 'I gather that German is spelled as you pronounce it. Curious, but there we are.'

'So how do you spell Plank?' asked Matthew Gurewitsch.

'Haughland,' said Plank.

Von Igelfeld could not conceal his astonishment. 'Haughland?'

'Indeed,' said Haughland (*voce*, Plank). 'It's an old family from the eastern fens somewhere. Virtually in the water.'

'But your humour remained dry,' observed Matthew Gurewitsch.

This remark brought silence, which was only broken when Dr C. A. D. Wood rose to her feet to leave.

'I have to go, Plank,' she said curtly. And then, more genially: 'Good afternoon, Professor von Igelfeld. Good afternoon, Mr Gurewitsch. I look forward to seeing you at dinner.'

That afternoon, von Igelfeld spent several very rewarding hours with the Hughes-Davitt Bequest before returning to his rooms to write a letter to Prinzel.

'This is an extraordinary place,' he wrote. 'Nothing is as it seems. However, I am immensely pleased with the Library and with the Hughes-Davitt Bequest, which has some first-rate material, wasted in this country, if you ask me; it would be far better looked after in Germany. However, at least I can put it into some sort of order and I shall eventually publish a paper on it. So my time here will be well-spent.

'However, there is the issue of my colleagues. So far I have not met one, not one, who would survive in a proper German academic institution, apart from the other visitor at the moment, Mr Matthew Gurewitsch from New York. He is very well-informed and has a fund of information about operatic matters. I fear that he may not be properly appreciated here, but we shall see what sort of response he gets to his lecture at the beginning of next week. Poor man! The mathematicians and the like who live in the College are unlikely to understand what he has to say; for the most part their minds are taken up with mathematical disputes and with plotting against one another. This has made the Master a nervous wreck, and indeed he is close to tears most of the time.

'How I long to be back in Germany, where everything is so solid and dependable. How I long to be back in the Institute common room, exchanging views with my colleagues. I am even missing Unterholzer, although I cannot quite bring myself to write to him yet. Perhaps next week. Please make sure, by the way, that he does not try to take my room while I am away. I know that he would like to do this, as he has done it in the past. I am counting on you to see that it does not happen.

'In this pallid land, then, I remain, Your friend eternally, Moritz-Maria von Igelfeld.'

He posted the letter in the College post-box, and then, it being a pleasant evening, he went for a stroll through the Fellows' Garden and out along the river. The Fellows' Garden was peaceful, in a way that only an English garden can be peaceful, and even the thought of de Courcey's detached skull did not disturb the feeling of *rus in urbe* which the garden encouraged. He found the giant wisteria bush which the Master had mentioned, and he found, too, a magnificent fuchsia hedge which ran along the southern boundary of the garden. There were benches, too, carved stone benches on which weary Fellows might sit and enjoy the flowers and shrubs, and it was on one of these that von Igelfeld was seated when he heard footsteps on the gravel behind him. He turned round, jolted out of a pleasant reverie in which he was back in Italy, in Tuscany, with the smell of lavender and rosemary on the breeze. Dr C. A. D. Wood and Dr Hall were bearing down upon him along the small path that cut through the lavender beds.

'Ah, there you are Professor von Igelfeld,' said Dr C. A. D. Wood. 'Hall and I were hoping to find you. Dr Porter said that he had seen you through his binoculars – he likes to watch the garden, you know. Nothing better to do, I suppose.'

The two Fellows joined him on his bench. As they sat down, the bench tilted slightly in the direction of Dr Hall, and von Igelfeld had to move over quickly towards Dr C. A. D. Wood in order to stop the entire party being tipped over.

'You have a beautiful garden,' said von Igelfeld conversationally.

'Yes,' said Dr Hall. 'And I find it best at this time of year – very early autumn, even if the colour is diminishing somewhat.'

'It's a good place to talk,' said Dr C. A. D. Wood. 'There's no

[48]

chance of the Master interrupting one's conversation. He suffers from hay fever, and so this is the place where we go when we need to talk about anything important.'

'I would not wish to prevent you,' said von Igelfeld, beginning to rise to his feet.

Dr C. A. D. Wood pulled him back on to the bench. 'No,' she said. 'Please don't go. We actually wanted to talk to you, didn't we, Hall?'

Dr Hall nodded. 'That's why we came out here. We wanted to have a quiet word with you.'

Von Igelfeld said nothing. Was this the plotting which the Master had warned him about?

'It's about the Augusta lecture,' said Dr C. A. D. Wood. 'The opera lecture.'

'I am looking forward to it immensely,' said von Igelfeld. 'Mr Matthew Gurewitsch has some very interesting ideas. I suspect that he will be controversial.'

'Oh yes,' said Dr C. A. D. Wood quickly. 'He was a good choice. That's why I hope that he has the chance to deliver his lecture.'

Von Igelfeld was confused. Why should there be any question about that? Mr Matthew Gurewitsch had arrived safely from New York and was all prepared to deliver the lecture, which he had already discussed with von Igelfeld. He could not see why any difficulties should arise.

Sensing his confusion, Dr C. A. D. Wood continued. 'The problem is that there are those who are keen to stop the lecture from taking place. There are those who are implacably opposed to opera on ideological grounds. They want the lecture to be more socially relevant. They want the money so kindly left by Count

Augusta to be used for the advancement of knowledge in a quite different sphere – agricultural economics, for example. They seem to object in some way to the fact that the money was made from a helicopter factory near Bologna.'

She paused, watching von Igelfeld for his reaction.

'But that's outrageous,' burst out von Igelfeld. 'What possible difference does it make that Count Augusta had a helicopter factory? That is quite irrelevant, I would have thought.'

Dr Hall nodded vigorously. 'Somebody has to make helicopters,' he pointed out.

'Exactly,' said von Igelfeld. 'But quite apart from that, their objection disturbs the settled intention of Count Augusta, who surely had the right to decide what his money should be used for. That is a point of principle.'

'Principle,' echoed Dr Hall, tapping the edge of the stone bench with a slightly fleshy finger.

'It would also be discourteous, to say the least,' continued von Igelfeld, 'for the invitation to Mr Matthew Gurewitsch to be withdrawn at this late stage, or indeed at any stage, once it had been issued.'

'Our thoughts precisely,' said Dr Hall unctuously, smoothing his hair as he did so. 'It's quite unacceptable behaviour, in our view.'

'But who can be behind it?' asked von Igelfeld. 'Who could possibly dream up something so base?'

'Plank,' said Dr C. A. D. Wood in a quiet voice.

'Haughland (Plank),' said Dr Hall. 'Haughland is Chairman of the Fellows' Committee. It's a very influential position, and if the Fellows' Committee decides to cancel Mr Matthew Gurewitsch's lecture, then there's nothing anybody can do about it.'

'But surely the Committee would never agree to that,' protested von Igelfeld. 'There must be other members who would vote against such a suggestion.'

Dr Hall nodded his agreement. 'Yes, there are other members, but they are weak. The Master, for instance, is on the Committee, but he always votes with Plank because Plank is in a position to blackmail him over something or other which happened years ago. So he would never stand up to him. Then there's Dr Porter, who lives in a world of his own imagination and who simply can't be predicted, either way. And Dr McGrew, who owes Plank money, and so on. So you see that even if the majority of the Fellows are against Plank, he happens to control that Committee.'

Von Igelfeld's face darkened as this perfidious story was un-ravelled. Such events would never have happened in Germany, but now nothing in England would surprise him. He was appalled at the prospect of Matthew Gurewitsch's invitation being with-drawn, and he blushed for the shamelessness of his new colleagues. Although he was only a visiting professor, he felt that he would be tarnished to be associated with an institution that could behave in such a way. And yet what could he do?

'Something can be done, of course,' said Dr C. A. D. Wood. 'We could call an extraordinary meeting of the Fellows and elect a new Committee, replacing Haughland with somebody else. Perhaps myself even. I would be prepared, if pressed. For the sake of the College, of course.'

'But we would need every vote we could get,' interjected Hall. 'It would be that close. And I must say that, if similarly pressed, I would be prepared to take over responsibility for the College cellars. Nobody could argue that the Senior Tutor has done a decent job, even though he spends half his time in Bordeaux.'

'But we don't want to press you,' said Dr C. A. D. Wood. 'We just thought that we would mention the whole thing to you so that you would not be too disappointed if Mr Matthew Gurewitsch's lecture were to be cancelled. You obviously got on well with him. We saw you deep in conversation. We knew you'd be appalled to hear what Plank was up to.'

'I am,' said von Igelfeld. 'I am completely appalled. I can assure you that I shall vote in the way you suggest.'

'That's very good,' said Dr C. A. D. Wood, rising briskly from the bench. Dr Hall rose too, thus avoiding imbalance.

'The meeting will be tomorrow,' said Dr Hall. 'By our calculation, your vote clinches the matter. If you had said no, then it would have been an exact tie. That would have required the Master to exercise a casting vote, and that would have gone to Plank, because of the blackmail factor.'

'I am very glad you confided in me,' said von Igelfeld. 'It seems that I shall be able to help avert a dreadful situation.'

'Absolutely,' said Dr C. A. D. Wood. 'And here's another thing. Once we have the new Committee in place, we could put you in the Senior Tutor's quarters for the rest of your stay. He can move to his old rooms, near the kitchen. I wouldn't need the Senior Tutor's rooms myself, as I have perfectly good rooms of my own. But that would mean that you would be very comfortable up there, with your own bathroom.'

Von Igelfeld smiled with pleasure. 'And then perhaps Mr Matthew Gurewitsch could have my current rooms and consequently more immediate access to that shared bathroom.'

'That would be perfectly feasible,' said Dr Hall. 'All of this will become possible once we get rid of Plank.'

That evening there was a College Feast, it being the anniversary of the beheading of the Founder. Von Igelfeld found this information unsettling, as he had spent much of his time in the Fellows' Garden, prior to the arrival of Drs C. A. D. Wood and Hall, reflecting on the melancholy fate of William de Courcey and on the question of his head's current location. He had reached no conclusions on the matter, other than that mankind's moral progress was slow, and intermittent. People still lost their heads, here and there in the world, but not, thank God, in Western Europe any longer. That was no solution to the troubles of the rest of the world, which were enough, when one contemplated them, to make one weep, just as the Master wept. Perhaps the College was a microcosm of the world at large, and when the Master burst into tears of despair he was weeping for the whole world. That was possible, but the analogy would require a great deal of further thought and for the moment there was the smell of the lavender and the delicate branches of the wisteria.

Von Igelfeld was pleased to discover that at the Feast he was placed just two seats away from Mr Matthew Gurewitsch, and was able to join in the conversation that the opera writer was having with Mr Max Wilkinson, who had been seated between them. Mr Wilkinson, although a mere mathematician, proved to have a lively interest in opera and a knowledge that matched this interest. He quizzed Matthew Gurewitsch on the forthcoming production of the *Ring* cycle, in miniature, at Glyndebourne, and Mr Gurewitsch expressed grave concern about miniaturisation of Wagner, a concern which von Igelfeld strongly endorsed.

'You have to be careful,' said Matthew Gurewitsch. 'You reduce the Rhine to a birdbath, and is there room, realistically speaking, for the Rhine Maidens, if that happens?'

[53]

'Exactly,' said von Igelfeld. 'And Valhalla too. What becomes of Valhalla?'

'It could become a sort of dentist's waiting room,' said Matthew Gurewitsch. 'No, you may laugh, but I have seen that happen. I saw a production once which made Valhalla just that. I shall spare the producer's blushes by not telling you who he was. But can you imagine it?'

'Why would the gods choose to live in a dentist's waiting room?' asked von Igelfeld.

There was a sudden silence at the table. This question had been asked during a lull in the conversation in other quarters, and it echoed loudly through the Great Hall. Even the undergraduates heard it, and paused, forks and spoons halfway to their mouths. Then, with no satisfactory answer forthcoming from the general company, the noisy hubbub of conversation resumed. Von Igelfeld noticed, however, that Dr C. A. D. Wood had shot a glance at Dr Hall, who had made a sign of some sort to her.

'They wouldn't,' said Matthew Gurewitsch, looking up at the intricate hammer-beam ceiling. 'It's the desire for novel effect. But there should be limits.' He paused, before adding: 'There are other objections to miniaturisation. The size of some singers, for example.'

'They cannot be made any smaller,' observed Mr Wilkinson.

'No,' said Matthew Gurewitsch. 'And there are always problems with size in opera. Mimi, for example, is rarely small and delicate. She is often sung by a lady who is very large and who, quite frankly, *simply doesn't look consumptive*. But at least we can suspend disbelief in such cases – within the conventions. But we should not create new challenges to our disbelief.'

'Absolutely not,' said von Igelfeld.

The conversation continued in this pleasant vein. Matthew

Gurewitsch alluded to the interferences with *Trovatore*, which he intended to expose in his lecture.

'Satires of *Trovatore* merely scratch the surface,' he said, 'leaving its mythic core untouched.'

'I would agree,' said von Igelfeld.

Matthew Gurewitsch smiled. 'Thank you. *Il Trovatore* is to opera nothing less than what *Oedipus Rex* is to spoken drama: the revelation of the soul of tragedy in its purest form. In both, ancient secrets unravel, devastating the innocent along with the guilty. But then, who is innocent?'

Von Igelfeld looked down the table towards Plank, who was sitting next to a woman who had been at dinner the previous evening, but to whom von Igelfeld had not been introduced. She was engaged in conversation with Plank, and had laid a hand briefly on his forearm, only to remove it almost immediately. Plank was smiling, and for a moment von Igelfeld was filled with a form of pure moral horror. How could he sit there, in full dissemblance, at the same table as the proposed victim of his plot? No Florentine painter could have captured the essence of Judas's table manners more clearly than flesh and blood that evening portrayed them in the form of Dr Plank, or so von Igelfeld reflected.

Matthew Gurewitsch, unaware of the peril which faced him, continued. 'In the tragic no-man's land between reason and unreason, the great crime is to have been born, would you not agree?'

'Yes,' said von Igelfeld. 'I would.'

'At that, a man may go to the grave never having known who he is,' continued Matthew Gurewitsch. 'Which is almost – almost, but not quite – what happened to Oedipus.'

There was more to be said on this subject, and it was said that evening. There were toasts as well, one to the Master – proposed by the Senior Tutor, who modestly praised the wine, his choice, before glasses were raised – and one to the Memory of the Founder. The Master then rose to give a short address.

'Dear guests of the College,' he began, 'dear Fellows, dear undergraduate members of this Foundation: William de Courcey was cruelly beheaded by those who could not understand that it is quite permissible for rational men to differ on important points of belief or doctrine. The world in which he lived had yet to develop those qualities of tolerance of difference of opinion which we take for granted, but which we must remind ourselves is of rather recent creation and is by no means assured of universal support. There are amongst us still those who would deny to others the right to hold a different understanding of the fundamental issues of our time. Thus, if we look about us, we see dogma still in conflict with rival dogma; we see people of one culture or belief still at odds with their human neighbours who are of a different culture or belief; and we see many who are prepared to act upon this difference to the extent of denying the humanity of those with whom they differ. They are prepared to kill them, and innocent others in the process, in order to strike at those whom they perceive to be their enemies, even if these so-called enemies are, like them, simple human beings, with families that love them, and with hopes and fears about their own individual futures.

'How might William de Courcey, by some thought experiment visiting the world today, recognise those self-same conflicts and sorrows which marred his own world and made it such a dangerous and, ultimately for him, such a fatal place? He would, I suspect, say that much has remained the same; that even if we have put some of the agents of division and intolerance to flight, there is still much evidence of their work among us.

'Here in this place of learning, let us remind ourselves of the possibility of combating, in whatever small way we can, those divisions that come between man and man, between woman and woman, so that we may recognise in each other that vulnerable humanity that informs our lives, and makes life so precious; so that each may find happiness in his or her life, and in the lives of others. For what else is there for us to hope for? What else, I ask you, what else?'

The Master sat down, and there was a complete silence. Nobody spoke, nor coughed, nor murmured, nor otherwise disturbed the quiet which had fallen upon the room. At the end of the Hall, the portrait of William de Courcey was illuminated by the light of the many candles which had been placed upon the tables. His expression, fixed in oils, was a calm one, and his gaze went out, out beyond the High Table, and into that darkness that was both real, and metaphorical.

After a few minutes of silence, the Master rose to his feet, to lead the procession out of the Hall. Von Igelfeld noticed that there had been tears in his eyes, but that he had now wiped them away. They processed, still in silence, although now there was the sound of the scraping of chair legs on stone as the undergraduates rose to their feet to mark the departure of the High Table party. They too had been moved by the Master's words, and there were hearts there that had changed, and would never be the same again. In the Senior Common Room, the Fellows moved to their accustomed seats, around the flickering of the great log fire which de Courcey's will had stipulated should always be provided 'to warm the hearts of the Fellows and the poor scholars of the Foundation'. The poor scholars were excluded, of course, but the other part of the injunction had been honoured.

Von Igelfeld found himself seated next to Dr C. A. D. Wood,

who had Dr Hall at her other side. Plank was placed between Matthew Gurewitsch and the Senior Tutor.

Sipping at his coffee, von Igelfeld glanced at Dr C. A. D. Wood. She had no coffee cup in her hand, and was staring down at the floor, as if trying to read some message in the carpet. After a moment or two, she turned to Dr Hall, who had been staring miserably at the ceiling.

'I cannot proceed,' said Dr C. A. D. Wood suddenly, turning to von Igelfeld as she spoke. 'After those words of the Master's, I cannot continue with our plan. I am grievously sorry, Professor von Igelfeld. I misled you this afternoon. What I said about Plank was not true. There was no plan to cancel Mr Gurewitsch's lecture. He would never have done that. He is a good man, and I have been seduced, yes seduced, by my personal ambition, into misrepresenting his intentions. I can only ask your forgiveness.'

Von Igelfeld listened intently to this confession. He, too, had been greatly affected by the Master's address, but it had never occurred to him that Dr C. A. D. Wood and Dr Hall would have been the centre of such a perfidious plot.

Dr Hall now spoke, turning to von Igelfeld and fixing him with a mournful stare. 'What she says is correct,' he said. 'We have behaved very badly. Along with others, who I hope are feeling just as bad as we are. I am only sorry that it has taken a Road to Damascus to reveal to us just how wicked we have been.'

Von Igelfeld reached forward and placed his coffee cup on the table before him. 'And I have behaved badly too,' he said. 'I too have been obliged to consider my own actions.'

'Oh?' said Dr C. A. D. Wood. 'What did you do? Was it something to do with Plank?'

'No,' said von Igelfeld. 'But it was to do with Mr Gurewitsch.'

He paused, plucking up his courage. 'I told him that there was no bathroom on our stair. I told him that he would have to cross the Court. And that was all because I didn't want another person sharing the bathroom with Professor Waterfield and myself. I did not actually lie, but I as good as lied.'

Dr Hall shook his head. 'That's the problem with these old buildings,' he said. 'There just aren't enough bathrooms.'

'Well, that may be so,' said von Igelfeld. 'But it doesn't excuse my action. I shall have to tell him immediately after coffee.'

'And we shall tell the others that there will be no emergency meeting called tomorrow,' said Dr C. A. D. Wood. 'And I shall say something decent to Plank.'

'Absolutely,' said Dr Hall. 'I propose to go straight over to him, right now, and tell him that I think that he's doing a very good job as Chairman of the Council.'

'That will please him,' said Dr C. A. D. Wood. 'Nobody's ever said anything like that to him before. Poor Haughland (*voce*, Plank).'

At the end of coffee, as the Fellows broke up for the evening, von Igelfeld made his way over to join Matthew Gurewitsch, who was examining one of the College portraits, a picture of a former Master, who had been beheaded under Cromwell.

'Mr Gurewitsch,' said von Igelfeld. 'I owe you an apology. I omitted to tell you that there was a bathroom at the top of the stairs and that you could use it.'

It was not an easy confession for von Igelfeld to make, but at least it was quick in the making.

'Oh that,' said Matthew Gurewitsch. 'Yes, don't worry. I found it. I've been using it all along. Do you use it as well?' he paused. 'In fact, I must confess I've been feeling rather guilty about it. I wondered if I should be telling others about it.'

Von Igelfeld laughed. 'That makes it easier for me,' he said.

They walked across the Court together. The atmosphere in the College seemed lighter now, as if a cloud of some sort had been dispelled.

'You know,' said von Igelfeld. 'Walking in these marvellous surroundings puts one in mind of opera, does it not? This setting. These ancient buildings.'

'It certainly does,' said Matthew Gurewitsch. 'Perhaps I shall write a libretto about a Cambridge college. In fact, I seem quite inspired. The ideas are coming to me already.'

'Would it be possible for me to be in it?' asked von Igelfeld. 'I would not want a large role, but if it were just possible for . . . '

'Of course,' said Mathew Gurewitsch. 'And it will be a fine role too. Positively heroic.'

Von Igelfeld said nothing. The Master had been right; the world was a distressing place, but there were places of light within it, not tiny particles of light like the quarks and bosons which the physicists chased after, but great bursts of light, like healing suns.

AT THE VILLA OF
REDUCED CIRCUMSTANCES

O N HIS RETURN FROM SABBATICAL in Cambridge –
a period of considerable achievement in his scholarly
career – Professor Dr Moritz-Maria von Igelfeld, author of that
most exhaustive work of Romance philology, *Portuguese Irregular
Verbs*, lost no time in resuming his duties at the Institute.
Although von Igelfeld was delighted to be back in Germany, he
had enjoyed Cambridge, especially after the Master's address had
so effectively stopped all that divisive plotting. Mr Matthew
Gurewitsch's lecture had been well-attended and well-received,
with several Fellows describing it as the most brilliant exposition
of an issue which they had heard for many years. Von Igelfeld had
taken copious notes, and had later raised several points about the
interpretation of *Il Trovatore* with Mr Matthew Gurewitsch, all
of which had been satisfactorily answered. In the weeks that
followed, he had struck up a number of close friendships, not
only with those repentant schemers, Dr C. A. D. Wood and Dr
Gervaise Hall, but also with their intended victim, Dr Plank.

Plank revealed himself to be both an agreeable man and a
conscientious and competent Chairman of the College Committee.
He invited von Igelfeld to tea in his rooms on several occasions, and

even took him back to his house to meet his wife, the well-known potter, Hermione Plank-Harwood. Professor Waterfield, too, proved to be a generous host, taking von Igelfeld for lunch at his London club, the Savile. Von Igelfeld was intrigued by this club, which appeared to have no purpose, as far as he could ascertain, and which could not be explained in any satisfactory terms by Professor Waterfield. Von Igelfeld asked him why he belonged, and Professor Waterfield simply shrugged. 'Because it's there, my dear chap,' he said lightly. 'Same reason Mallory wanted to climb Everest. Because it was there. And I wonder whether Sherpa Tenzing climbed it because *Hillary* was there?'

'I find that impossible to answer,' said von Igelfeld. 'And the initial proposition is in every sense unconvincing. You don't climb mountains just because they're there.'

'I agree with you,' said Professor Waterfield. 'But that's exactly what Mallory said about Everest. *Ipse dixit*. I would never climb a mountain myself, whether or not it was there. Although I might be more tempted to climb one that wasn't there, if you see what I mean.'

'No,' said von Igelfeld. 'I do not. And I cannot imagine why one would join a club just because it is there. The club must do something.'

'Not necessarily,' said Professor Waterfield. 'And actually, old chap, would you mind terribly if we brought this line of conversation to a close? It's just that one of the rules of this place' – this was at lunch in the Savile – 'one of the rules is that you aren't allowed to discuss the club's *raison d'être* in the club itself. Curious rule, but there we are. Perhaps it's because it unsettles the members. London, by the way, is full of clubs that have no real reason to exist. Some more so than others. I've never been able to work out why Brooks's exists, quite frankly, and then there's the Athenaeum, which is for bishops and intellectual poseurs. I suppose they have to go somewhere. But that's hardly a reason to establish a club for them.'

Von Igelfeld was silent. There were aspects of England that he would never understand, and this, it seemed, was one of them. Perhaps the key was to consider it a tribal society and to under-stand it as would an anthropologist. In fact, the more he thought of that, the more apt the explanation became, and later, when he put it to Professor Waterfield himself, the Professor nodded enthusiastically.

'But of course that's the right way to look at this country,' he said. 'They should send anthropologists from New Guinea to live amongst us. They could then write their Harvard PhDs on places like this club, and the university too.' He paused. 'Could the same not be said of Germany?'

'Of course not,' said von Igelfeld sharply; the idea was absurd. Germany was an entirely rational society, and the suggestion that it might be analysed in anthropological terms was hardly a serious one. It was typical of Professor Waterfield's conversation, he thought, which in his view was a loosely-held-together stream of non sequiturs and unsupported assertions. That's what came of being Anglo-Saxon, he assumed, instead of being German; the *Weltanschauung* of the former was, quite simply, wrong.

He arrived back in Germany on a Sunday afternoon, which gave him time to attend to one or two matters before getting back to work on the Monday morning. There was a long letter from Zimmermann which had to be answered – that was a priority – and von Igelfeld wrote a full reply that Sunday evening. Zimmermann was anxious to hear about Cambridge, and to get news of some of the friends whom he had made during his year there. How was

Haughland (Plank)? Had Dr Mauve finished writing his riposte to the review article which Nenée-Franck had so unwisely published in the *Revue Comparative de Grammaire Contemporaine* the year before last? He should not leave it too late, said Zimmermann: false interpretations can enter the canon if not dealt with in a timely fashion and then can prove almost impossible to uproot. And what about the Hughes-Davitt Bequest? What were von Igelfeld's preliminary conclusions, and would they appear reasonably soon in the *Zeitschrift*? Von Igelfeld went through each of these queries carefully, and was able to give Zimmermann much of the information he sought.

He made an early start in the Institute the next morning, arriving even before the Librarian, who was usually the first to come in, well in advance of anybody else. The Librarian greeted him with warmth.

'Professor von Igelfeld!' he exclaimed. 'It is so wonderful to have you back. Do you know, only yesterday, my aunt asked after you! You will recall that some months before you went to Cambridge you had asked me to pass on to her your best regards. I did that, immediately, the very next time that I went to the nursing home. She was very touched that you had remembered her and she was very concerned when she heard that you had to go off to Cambridge. She said that she was worried that you would not be well looked after there, but I assured her that there was no danger of this. It's odd, isn't it, how that generation worries about things like that? You and I would have no hesitation about leaving Germany for foreign parts, but they don't like it. It's something to do with insecurity. I think that my aunt feels a certain degree of insecurity because she . . . '

'Yes, yes, Herr Huber,' von Igelfeld interrupted. 'That is very

true. Now, I was wondering whether anything of note had happened in the Institute during my absence.'

The Librarian looked thoughtful. 'It depends on what you mean by the expression "of note". If "of note" means "unusual", then the answer, I fear, is no. Nothing unusual has happened – in the strict sense of the word. If, however, "of note" is synonymous with "of importance", which is the meaning which I, speaking entirely personally, would be inclined to attribute to it, in the main, then one might conceivably come up with a different answer. Yes, that would probably be the case, although I could never really say *ex Germania semper aliquid novi*, if you will allow the little joke . . . '

'Very amusing,' said von Igelfeld quickly. 'Except for the fact that one should say *e Germania*, the *ex* form, as you know, being appropriate before a vowel, hence, *ex Africa* in the original. Be that as it may, certainly far more amusing than anything I heard in Cambridge. I'm afraid it's true, you know, that the British don't have a sense of humour.'

'I've heard that said,' agreed the Librarian. 'Very humourless people.'

'But if I may return to the situation here,' pressed von Igelfeld. '*Ex institutione aliquid novi?*'

The Librarian smiled. He knew exactly what von Igelfeld would be interested in, which would be whether anybody had requested a copy of *Portuguese Irregular Verbs* in his absence. Normally, the answer to this would be a disappointing negative, but this time there was better news to impart, and the Librarian was relishing the prospect of revealing it. But he did not want to do it too quickly; with skilful manipulation of von Igelfeld's questions, he might be able to keep the information until coffee, when he could reveal it in the presence of everybody. They were always cutting him short when he had something interesting to say; well, if they tried that today, then they would have to do so in the face of very evident and strong interest on the part of von Igelfeld.

Oh yes, the world is unjust, thought the Librarian. They – Prinzel, Unterholzer and von Igelfeld (Zimmermann, too, come to think of it) – had all the fun. They went off to conferences and meetings all over the place and he had to stay behind in the Library, all day, every day. All he had to look forward to each evening was the visit to the nursing home and the short chat with the nurses and with his aunt. It was always a pleasure to talk to his aunt, of course, who was so well-informed and took such an interest in everything, but afterwards he had to go back to his empty apartment and have his dinner all by himself. He had been married, and happily so, he had imagined, until one day his wife walked out on him with absolutely no notice. She had met a man who rode a motorcycle on a Wall of Death at a funfair, and she had decided that she preferred him to the Librarian. He had tracked her down to a site outside Frankfurt – the sort of wasteland which funfairs like to occupy – and he had had a brief and impassioned conversation with her outside the Wall of Death while her motorcyclist lover raced round and round inside. He had implored her to come back, but his words were lost in the roar of the motorcycle engine and in the rattling of the brightly painted wooden planks that made up the outside of the Wall of Death.

Such was the Librarian's life. But at least von Igelfeld was kind to him, and it would give him very great pleasure to tell him, when the moment was right, that a copy of *Portuguese Irregular Verbs* had been requested, and despatched, to none other than Señor Gabriel Marcales de Cinco Fermentaciones, cultural attaché at the Colombian Embassy. This was remarkable news, and although he could not say with certainty what it implied, it undoubtedly had interesting possibilities.

'Yes,' he said to von Igelfeld. 'I believe that there is something which will interest you. I shall obtain the details – I do not have them on me right now – and I shall tell you about it over coffee.'

During the hours before coffee, von Igelfeld busied himself in his room, going through the circulars and other correspondence that his secretary had not deemed sufficiently weighty to send on to Cambridge. Most of this was completely unimportant and required no response, but there were one or two matters which needed to be addressed. There was a request from a student in Berlin that he be allowed to work in the Institute for a couple of months over summer. Von Igelfeld was dubious; students had a way of creating a great deal of extra work and were, in general, the bane of a professor's life. That was why so few German professors saw any students; it was regrettable, but necessary if one's time was to be protected from unacceptable encroachments. On the other hand, this young man could be useful, and could, in the fullness of time, become an assistant. So von Igelfeld wrote a guarded reply, inviting the student for an interview. That task performed, he set himself to a far more important piece of business, which was to discover evidence of Unterholzer's having been in his room during his absence.

Von Igelfeld knew that Unterholzer could be cunning, particularly when it came to issues of rooms and chairs. He would not have done anything so unwise as to have left a sign on the door with his name on it; nor would he have moved any of the furniture. Of course, one could check the position of the chairs and possibly find that one or two had been shifted very slightly from their original position, but this was not proof of any significance, as the cleaners often moved things when they were cleaning the room. There were other potential clues: the number of paper-clips in the paper-clip container was a possibility, but then again Unterholzer would have been aware of this and would have made sure that he had replaced any such items.

Von Igelfeld looked closely at the large square of framed blotting paper on his desk. This was the surface on which he normally wrote, and if Unterholzer had done the same, then one might expect to find evidence in the form of the inked impression of Unterholzer's script. He picked up the blotter and examined it carefully. He had not had the foresight to insert a fresh sheet of paper before he left, and the existing sheet had numerous markings of his own. It was difficult to make out what was what, as everything was reversed. Von Igelfeld paused. If one held the blotter up to a mirror, then the ink marks would be reversed and everything would be easily readable.

He made his way quickly to the men's washroom, where there was a large mirror above a row of hand-basins. Switching on the light in the darkened room, he held the blotter up to the mirror and began to study it. There was his signature, or part of it, in the characteristic black ink which he used: M . . . . . M . . . . von Ige . f . . d. And there was half a line of a letter which he recalled writing to Zimmermann almost six months ago. That was all legitimate, as were most of the other markings; most, but not all: what was this? It was clearly not in his handwriting and, if he was not mistaken, it was Unterholzer's well-known sprawling script. Moreover, and this suggested that no further proof would be needed, the blotting was in green ink, which was the colour which Unterholzer, and nobody else in the Institute, used.

'I have my proof,' muttered von Igelfeld under his breath. 'The sheer effrontery of it!'

It was at this point that the Librarian entered the washroom. He stood in the doorway, momentarily taken aback at the sight of von Igelfeld holding the blotter up to the mirror.

'Professor von Igelfeld!' he exclaimed. 'May I help you in some way?'

Confused and embarrassed, von Igelfeld rapidly dropped the blotter to his side. 'I have been looking at this blotter in the mirror,' he said.

'So I see,' said the Librarian.

For a few moments nothing further was said. Then von Igelfeld continued: 'I am in the habit of making notes to myself – memoranda, you understand – and I have unfortunately lost one. I am searching for some trace of it.'

'Ah!' said the Librarian. 'I understand. It must be very frustrating. And it would appear that poor Professor Dr Unterholzer must suffer from the very same difficulty. A few months ago I came across him in here doing exactly this, reading a blotter in the mirror!'

Von Igelfeld stared at the Librarian. This was information of the very greatest significance.

'This blotter?' he asked. 'Reading this very blotter?'

The Librarian glanced at the blotter which von Igelfeld now held out before him. 'I can't say whether it was that one exactly. But certainly something similar.'

Von Igelfeld narrowed his eyes. This made the situation even more serious; not only had Unterholzer used his room in his absence, but he had tried to read what he, the unwilling host, had written. This was an intolerable intrusion, and he would have to confront Unterholzer and ask him why he saw fit to pry into the correspondence of others. Of course, Unterholzer would deny it, but he would know that von Igelfeld knew, and that would surely deprive him of any pleasure he had obtained from poking his nose into von Igelfeld's affairs.

Von Igelfeld returned to his room in a state of some indignation. He replaced the blotter on his desk and looked carefully around his room. What would be required now was a thorough search, just in case there was any other evidence of Unterholzer's presence. One never knew; if he had been so indiscreet as to read the blotter in the washroom, knowing that anybody might walk in on him, then he may well have left some other piece of damning evidence.

Von Igelfeld examined his bookshelves closely. All his books, as far as he could ascertain, were correctly shelved. He looked in the drawer which held his supply of paper and ink; again, everything seemed to be in order. Then, as he closed the drawer, his eye fell on a small object on the carpet – a button.

Von Igelfeld stooped down and picked up the button. He examined it closely: it was brown, small, and gave no indication of its provenance. But his mind was already made up: here was the proof he needed. This button was a very similar shade to the unpleasant brown suits which Unterholzer wore. This was undoubtedly an Unterholzer button, shed by Unterholzer during his clandestine tenancy of von Igelfeld's room. Von Igelfeld slipped the button into his pocket. He would produce it at coffee so that everybody could notice – and share – Unterholzer's discomfort.

When von Igelfeld arrived in the coffee room, the others were already seated around the table, listening to a story which Prinzel was telling.

'When I was a young boy,' Prinzel said, 'we played an enchanting game – Greeks and Turks. It was taught us by our own nursemaid, a Greek girl, who came to work for the family when she was sixteen. I believe that she had played the game on her native Corfu. The rules were such that the Greeks always won, and therefore we all wanted to be Greeks. It was not so much fun being a Turk, but somebody had to be one, and so we took it in turns.' He paused, thinking for a moment.

'What a charming game,' said the Librarian. 'My aunt tells me that when she was a girl they used to play with metal hoops. You would roll the hoop along the ground with a stick and run after it. Girls would tie ribbons to their sticks. Boys usually didn't. If your hoop started down a slope you might have to run very fast indeed! She said that one day a small boy who lived opposite them, a boy by the name of Hans, rolled his hoop into a tram line and the hoop began to roll towards an oncoming tram. My aunt told me that . . . '

'One of Professor Freud's patients was called Hans,' interjected Prinzel. 'He was called Little Hans. He was always worried that the dray-horses would bite him. His father consulted Professor Freud about this and Professor Freud wrote a full account of the case.'

The Librarian looked aggrieved. 'I do not think it can be the same boy. I was merely recounting . . . '

'My wife reads Freud for the sheer pleasure of the prose,' said Unterholzer. 'She received some training in psychology during her studies. I myself have not read Freud, but it's perfectly possible that I shall read him in the future. I have not ruled that out.'

'This boy with his hoop,' said the Librarian. 'It was stuck in the line and was rolling directly towards the tram. I think that this must have been in Munich, although it could have been in Stuttgart, because my aunt's father, my great-uncle, removed from Munich to Stuttgart when my aunt was eight, or was it seven? Eight, I think, but don't quote me on that. I might be wrong. But the point is that when a hoop gets into a tramline, then there is only one way for it to go. That's the problem. You can imagine if you were that boy's father and you saw the hoop stuck in the tramline. Well, the father was there, as it happened, and he ran . . . '

He stopped, not because he had been interrupted, but because von Igelfeld had arrived. Immediately they all stood, Prinzel reaching forward to shake von Igelfeld's hand, followed by Unterholzer, who smiled with pleasure as he did so. Von Igelfeld watched Unterholzer; such hypocrisy, he thought, but so well concealed. Well, the button would put an end to that.

They settled down to enjoy their coffee.

'It's wonderful to have you back,' said Prinzel. 'The Institute doesn't seem to be the same place when you're away.'

No, thought von Igelfeld, it wouldn't be, would it? There would be a different person in my room. But he did not give voice to such churlish doubts, instead he remarked brightly: 'I cannot tell you how happy I am to be back in Germany. Cambridge is a fine place, but you know the problem.'

They all nodded sympathetically. 'Four months in an inferior institution must be very difficult,' said Unterholzer. 'I expect you had a battle to get anything done.'

'Yes,' said von Igelfeld. 'Everything is so irrational in that country. And the people, quite frankly, are utterly eccentric. You have to analyse their smallest pronouncements to work out what they mean. If it is bad weather they will say things like, "Charming weather we're having!"'

'And yet the weather isn't charming,' said Unterholzer. 'Why then do they say that it's charming?'

'Why indeed?' agreed von Igelfeld. 'They often say the direct opposite of what they mean.'

'That's extremely strange,' said the Librarian. 'In fact, one might even describe that as pathological.'

'And then they consistently understate a position,' went on von Igelfeld. 'If they are very ill, or dying, they will say something like, "I'm feeling very slightly below par." It's very odd. You may recall Captain Oates going out of his tent into the Antarctic wastes. He knew that he would never come back. So what did he say? "I may be some time." This actually meant that he would never come back.'

'Then why didn't he say that?' asked Unterholzer.

Von Igelfeld shrugged his shoulders. 'It is something which I shall never understand,' he said. 'It is quite beyond reason.'

Prinzel smiled. 'It was just as well that you understood how to deal with these people, Captain Oates and his like,' he said. 'I should have been terribly confused.'

'Thank you,' said von Igelfeld. 'But in spite of all this, I did enjoy the experience.' He paused, and they waited. This was the moment. 'And of course it was a great reassurance to know that I had my room at the Institute to come back to.'

The silence was complete. Von Igelfeld did not look at Unterholzer, but he knew that his words had found their target. He would wait a few more seconds before he continued; if he waited too long, the Librarian might start talking about hoops or whatever and he did not want the dramatic impact of his find to be diminished.

He took a deep breath. 'Speaking of rooms, I found something in my room this morning. It was very puzzling.' He put his hand into his pocket, watched by all eyes, and extracted the button, holding it up for all to see. 'This.'

'A button,' said the Librarian. 'You found a button.'

'Precisely,' said von Igelfeld. 'A button on the carpet.'

They all stared at the button.

'This button,' said Prinzel. 'Is it an important button, or just . . . just a button?'

'You would have to ask that question of the person who dropped it,' said von Igelfeld slowly, each word chosen and delivered with care, so as to have maximum effect. 'That person – whoever it might be – would be able to answer your question. I cannot.'

Von Igelfeld still did not look directly at Unterholzer. He gazed, rather, out of the windows, at the bare branches of the trees, ready for the onset of spring. Those who deceived would always be found out, he reflected. We reap what we sow, or, in this case, what we drop. That, he thought, was quite amusing, but he should not laugh now, nor should he even smile. Perhaps he could express the thought later, in confidence, to Prinzel, or he could write to Zimmermann and put it in as an aside, as a freshly-minted aphorism. Zimmermann had a highly developed sense of humour and always appreciated such remarks.

Unterholzer put down his cup. 'Could you pass me the button, Herr von Igelfeld?' he said.

This tactic took von Igelfeld by surprise. Usually the accused does not ask to see the prosecution's principal exhibit, as he feels too embarrassed to handle it, fearing, perhaps, that he would not be able to conceal his familiarity with the object. But he could hardly refuse, and so he passed the button to its putative owner.

'Yes,' said Unterholzer, taking the button. 'Just as I thought. It's your own button, Herr von Igelfeld. If you look at the left sleeve of your jacket, you will see that there are only two buttons sewn on behind the cuff. On your right sleeve there are three. This button matches.the others. What good fortune that it fell off in your office and not outside. It could have fallen into a tramline and rolled away.'

At this last remark, Prinzel and Unterholzer burst into laughter, although the Librarian, inexplicably, did not. Von Igelfeld, humiliated, said nothing. He did not understand what tramlines had to do with it, and it was outrageous that Unterholzer should have wriggled out of his difficulties in this way. His one consolation was that Nemesis would take note, would stalk Unterholzer, and would trip him up one of these days. It was only a matter of time.

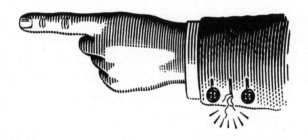

The Librarian realised that von Igelfeld was somehow put out by the way in which the button incident had been concluded, and decided that this would be the right time to mention the Colombian request. He did not like to see von Igelfeld humiliated, particularly when it was at the hands of his colleagues. They were so rude, sometimes; always interrupting him as if they were the only ones who had any right to speak. Well, now he would speak, and they would have to listen this time.

'Herr von Igelfeld,' he began. 'Putting buttons to one side – and who amongst us has not at some time shed a button, Herr Unterholzer? There is no shame in doing so, in my view. But be that as it may, there was a development while you were away. I thought I might mention it to you.'

Everybody looked at the Librarian, who for a few precious moments relished their evident anticipation. They could not interrupt him now.

'I had a request a month or so ago from a foreign embassy,' he said. 'A very particular request.'

The silence deepened. Unterholzer's lips were pursed, and von Igelfeld noticed that his hands were trembling slightly.

'Oh yes?' said von Igelfeld encouragingly. 'You alluded to something earlier on, Herr Huber. You have the details to hand now, I take it?'

The Librarian nodded. 'Yes, I do.' He paused, but only for a moment. 'The request came from the Colombian Embassy, in fact. They asked me for a copy of *Portuguese Irregular Verbs*, and I despatched one to them immediately. And . . . ' Now the tension was almost unbearable. 'And they asked me to provide a brief biographical note about yourself, *including any honours already received*, and to confirm the correct spelling of your name.'

The effect of these words was every bit as dramatic as the Librarian had anticipated. The information took a few moments to sink in, but when it had, all thoughts of buttons and such matters were replaced by a real and quite tangible sense of excitement. When all was said and done, what really mattered was the reputation of the Institute, and good news for one was good news for all. There may have been minor jealousies – and these were inevitable in philology – but when there was a whiff, even the merest whiff, of an honour from a foreign institution, then all such matters were swept aside. Now, in the face of this quite extraordinarily exciting news, the only thing that mattered was that they should find out, as soon as possible, what this development meant.

Prinzel was the first to suggest an explanation. 'I should imagine that it is an honorary degree from a Colombian university,' he said. 'There are some very prestigious institutions in Bogotá. The Rosario, for example, is very highly regarded in South America. It is a private university in Bogotá. I should think that is what it is. May I be the first to offer my congratulations, Herr von Igelfeld!'

Von Igelfeld raised a hand in a gesture of modesty. 'That could be quite premature, Herr Prinzel,' he protested. 'I cannot imagine that it will be an honour of any sort. I imagine that it is just for some small article in a government journal or newspaper. It will be no more than that.'

'Nonsense,' said the Librarian. 'They could get that sort of information from a press-cuttings agency. They would not need a copy of the book for that.'

'Herr Huber has a very good point,' said Unterholzer. 'There is more to this than meets the eye.'

'Please!' protested von Igelfeld. 'I would not wish to tempt Providence. You are all most generous in your assumptions, but I think it would be a grave error to think any more of this. Please let us talk about other matters. The *Zeitschrift*, for example. How is work progressing on the next issue? Have we sent everything off to the printer yet?'

His suggestion that they should think no more of this mysterious approach from the Colombian Embassy was, of course, not advice that he could himself follow. Over the next week, he thought of nothing else, flicking through each delivery of post to see whether there was a letter from Colombia or something that looked as if it came from the Colombian Embassy. And as for Prinzel and Unterholzer, they had several private meetings in which they discussed the situation at length, speculating as to whether they had missed any possible interpretation of the Embassy's request. They thought they had not. They had covered every possibility, and all of them looked good.

Eight days after the Librarian's announcement, the letter arrived. It was postmarked Bogotá, and von Igelfeld stared at it for a full ten minutes before he slit it open with his letter-knife and unfolded the heavy sheet of cotton-weave paper within. It was written in Spanish, a language of which he had a near perfect command, and it began by addressing him in that rather flowery way of South American institutions. The President of the Colombian Academy of Letters presented his compliments to the most distinguished Professor Dr von Igelfeld. From time to time, it went on, the Academy recognised the contribution of a foreign scholar, to whom it extended the privilege of Distinguished Corresponding Fellowship. This award was the highest honour which they could bestow and this year, 'in anticipation and in the strongest hope of a favourable response from your distinguished self', the Academy had decided to bestow this honour on von Igelfeld. There would be

a ceremony in Bogotá, which they hoped he would be able to attend.

He read the letter through twice, and then he stood up at his desk. He walked around the room, twice, allowing his elation to settle. Colombia! This was no mere Belgian honour, handed out indiscriminately to virtually anybody who bothered to visit Belgium; this came from the Academy of an influential South American state. He looked at his watch. Coffee time was at least an hour away and he had to tell somebody. He would write to Zimmermann, of course, but in the meantime he could start by telling the Librarian, who had played such an important role in all this. He found him alone in the Library, a sheaf of old-fashioned catalogue cards before him. After he had broken the news, he informed the Librarian that he was the first person to know of what had happened.

'Do you mean you haven't told the others?' asked the Librarian. 'You haven't even told Professor Dr Dr Prinzel yet?'

'No,' said von Igelfeld. 'I am telling you first.'

For a moment the Librarian said nothing. He stood there, at his card catalogue, looking down at the floor. There were few moments in his daily life which achieved any salience, but this, most surely, was one. Nobody told him anything. Nobody ever wrote to him or made him party to any confidence. Even his wife had not bothered to tell him that she was running away; if the building were to go on fire, he was sure that nobody would bother to advise him to leave. And now here was Professor Dr von Igelfeld, author of *Portuguese Irregular Verbs*, telling him, and telling him first, of a private letter he had received from the Colombian Academy of Letters.

'I am so proud, Herr von Igelfeld,' he said. 'I am so . . . ' He did not finish; there were no words strong enough to express his emotion.

'It is a joint triumph,' said von Igelfeld kindly. 'I would not have achieved this, Herr Huber, were it not for the constant support which I have received in my work from yourself. I am sure of that fact. I really am.'

'You are too kind, Herr von Igelfeld,' stuttered the Librarian. 'You are too kind to me.'

'It is no more than you deserve,' said von Igelfeld. A Corresponding Fellow of the Colombian Academy of Letters can always afford to be generous, and von Igelfeld was.

Not surprisingly, the arrangements for the bestowal of the honour proved to be immensely complicated. The cultural attaché was extremely helpful, but even with his help, the formalities were time-consuming. At last, after several months during which letters were exchanged on an almost weekly basis, the date of the ceremony was settled, and von Igelfeld's flight to Bogotá was booked. Señor

Gabriel Marcales de Cinco Fermentaciones, the cultural attaché, proposed to travel out with von Igelfeld, as he was being recalled to Bogotá anyway, and he thought that it would be convenient to accompany him and ensure a smooth reception at the other end.

Von Igelfeld was doubtful whether this was really necessary, but was pleased with the arrangement on two accounts. Cinco Fermentaciones, it transpired, was most agreeable company, being very well-informed on South American literary affairs. This alone would have made travelling together worthwhile, but there was more. When they arrived in Bogotá, there was no question of waiting at the airport for formalities; all of these were disposed of in the face of the diplomatic passport which the cultural attaché produced and with a letter which he folded and unfolded in the face of any official and which immediately seemed to open all doors. Von Igelfeld hesitated to ask what was in this letter, but Cinco Fermentaciones, seeing him looking at it with curiosity, offered an explanation of his own accord.

'I wrote it and signed it myself,' he said, with a smile. 'It says that I am to receive every assistance and consideration, and any request of mine is to be attended to with the utmost despatch. Then I stamped it with the Ambassador's stamp that he keeps on his desk and which seems to have quite magical properties. *Hola!* It works.'

Von Igelfeld was impressed, and wondered whether he might try the same tactic himself in future.

'Another example of South American magical realism,' said Señor Gabriel Marcales de Cinco Fermentaciones, with a laugh. 'Magical, but realistic at the same time.'

They travelled to von Igelfeld's hotel and Cinco Fermentaciones made sure that his guest was settled in before he left him. The letter was unfolded and displayed to the manager of the hotel, who nodded deferentially and gave von Igelfeld a quick salute in response. Then Cinco Fermentaciones promised to pick up von Igelfeld for the ceremony, which would take place at noon the following day.

'In the meantime, you can recover from the trip,' he said. 'This city is at a very great altitude, and you must take things easily.'

'Perhaps I shall take a look around later this afternoon,' said von Igelfeld, looking out of the window at the interesting Spanish colonial architecture of the surrounding streets.

Cinco Fermentaciones frowned. 'No,' he said. 'I wouldn't do that. Definitely not.'

Von Igelfeld was puzzled. 'But those buildings? May one not inspect them, even just from the outside?'

Cinco Fermentaciones shook his head. 'No,' he said. 'You must not leave the hotel. It is for your own safety.'

Von Igelfeld looked at the manager, who nodded his agreement with Cinco Fermentaciones and made a quick, but eloquent, throat-slitting gesture.

'Outside is extremely dangerous,' the manager said quietly. 'The whole country is extremely dangerous.'

'Surely not in the middle of the city,' protested von Igelfeld. 'Look, there are plenty of people outside in the streets.'

'Yes,' said Cinco Fermentaciones. 'And most of them are extremely dangerous. Believe me, I know my own country. Even this letter' – and he held up his potent document – 'even this wouldn't help you out there.'

'But who are these dangerous people?' asked von Igelfeld.

'Brigands, desperadoes, *narcotraficantes*, guerrillas,' began Cinco Fermentaciones. 'Extortionists, murderers, anti-Government factions, pro-Government factions, disaffected soldiers, corrupt policemen, revolutionary students, conservative students, students in general, cocaine producers, hostile small farmers, dispossessed peasants . . . And there are others.'

'Disaffected waiters as well,' interjected the hotel manager. 'We regularly receive bomb threats from a movement of disaffected waiters who attack hotels. It is very troublesome.'

Von Igelfeld said nothing. He had heard that Colombia was a troubled society, but he had imagined that the trouble was confined to lawless areas in the south. The way that Cinco Fermentaciones and the hotel manager were talking gave a very different impression. Was anybody safe in this country? Was the Academy of Letters itself safe, or were there disaffected writers who needed to be added to Cinco Fermentaciones' intimidating list? For a moment he wondered whether he should pose this question, but he decided, on balance, to leave it unasked.

In the face of this unambiguous advice, von Igelfeld remained within the confines of the hotel, venturing out only into the walled garden, where he sat for an hour, admiring a colourful display of red and blue bougainvillaea. That evening, after a light supper in the hotel dining room – a meal which he took in isolation, as there appeared to be no other guests – he slept fitfully, waking frequently through the night and anxiously checking that the door was still locked. There were strange noises in the corridor outside – a cough, the sound of footsteps, and at one point a muttered conversation, seemingly directly outside his door. In the morning, with the sun streaming through his window, the fears of the night receded, and he prepared himself with pleasurable anticipation for the day's events.

Cinco Fermentaciones called for him on time, dressed in a smart morning coat and sporting a carnation in his buttonhole.

'I hope that the night passed peacefully,' he said to von Igelfeld.

'Extremely peacefully,' replied von Igelfeld. This reply seemed to disappoint Cinco Fermentaciones, who made a gesture towards the door behind him.

'This country is unpredictable,' he said. 'One night is peaceful and then the next . . . Well, everything comes to a head.'

Von Igelfeld decided that he would not allow this pessimistic view to colour his experience of Colombia. Everyone in the hotel had been charming; the sun was shining benevolently; the air was crisp and clear. Cinco Fermentaciones could brood on political and social conflict if he wished; von Igelfeld, by contrast, was prepared to be more sanguine.

They set off for the premises of the Academy and ten minutes later arrived in front of a comfortable, colonial-style building in the old centre of Bogotá. There they were met by the President of the Academy, who came to the door to greet them. He was a distinguished-looking man in his late sixties, with a large moustache and round, unframed glasses. He led them into the Hall, where a group of about forty Members of the Academy, all formally dressed for the occasion, were seated in rows, every face turned towards the new Corresponding Fellow, every expression one of welcome.

'Most distinguished Academicians,' began the President, as he faced the membership. 'We have in our midst this morning one whose contribution to Romance philology has been exceeded by no other in the last one hundred years. When Professor von Igelfeld set aside his pen after writing the final sentence of that great work *Portuguese Irregular Verbs*, he may not have reflected on the fact that he had given the world a treasure of scholarship; a beacon to light the way of Romance philology in the years ahead. But that is what

Portuguese Irregular Verbs has been, and that is what it has done. All of us in this room are in his debt, and it is in recognition of this, that, by virtue of my powers as President of the Academy, I now confer Corresponding Fellowship on Professor Dr Moritz-Maria von Igelfeld, of the University of Heidelberg; *Magister Artium*, of the University of Göttingen; Doctor of Letters, of the Free University of Berlin; Member (third class) of the Order of Leopold of the Kingdom of Belgium.'

Von Igelfeld listened attentively as the roll of his honours and achievements was sonorously recited. It was a matter of regret, he felt, that the President saw fit to mention the Order of Leopold; he had accepted that before he realised that it was only third class (a fact which he had discovered at the installation ceremony) and he had tended therefore not to mention it. Herr Huber, as a librarian, was not one to allow a detail to escape his attention, and so he could not be blamed if he had listed it in the biographical information he had provided. After all, Herr Huber himself had nothing, and even a third-class award from the Belgians would have seemed worthwhile to him.

Von Igelfeld had little time for Belgium. In the first place, he was not at all sure that the country was even necessary, in the way in which France and Germany were obviously necessary. It would have been more convenient all round if part of Belgium had remained with France, as Napoleon had so wisely intended, and the Flemish part could then have been tacked on to the Netherlands, on linguistic grounds. And then there was the question of the Belgian monarchs, and in particular, Leopold, whose unapologetic behaviour in the Belgian Congo left a great deal to be desired. All in all, then, the Belgian order was something which was better not mentioned, although it was likely, on balance, to impress the Colombians.

The inauguration was simple: a medal was pinned to von Igelfeld's lapel, the President embraced him and kissed him on both cheeks, the large moustache tickling von Igelfeld's face, and then the Members of the Academy pressed forward to shake the hand of their new Corresponding Fellow. Thereafter, a light lunch was served, at which there was more hand-shaking, and the Members then dispersed. Von Igelfeld had prepared a lecture, just in case he should be asked to deliver one, but no opportunity presented itself. Nor did the President or any of the Members suggest that anything else should be done; the President, indeed, disappeared before von Igelfeld had the chance to thank him properly, and von Igelfeld found himself outside the Academy building, in the clear Andean sunshine, in the company only of Señor Gabriel Marcales de Cinco Fermentaciones.

'A moving ceremony,' said his host. 'I am not a Member of the Academy myself, although I feel that it would be very appropriate to be one.'

'I am sorry to hear that,' said von Igelfeld soothingly. 'But I am sure that somebody will propose you for membership one of these days.'

'I hope so,' said Cinco Fermentaciones. He paused, and looked at von Igelfeld. 'You wouldn't care to do that, would you?'

Von Igelfeld gave a start. 'I?' he said. 'I am only a Corresponding Fellow, and a new one at that. Surely it would be improper for me to propose a new member.'

'Not in the slightest,' said Cinco Fermentaciones. 'Indeed, it would be virtually impossible for them to turn me down if you proposed me. It would imply a lack of confidence in your judgement.' He reached into his pocket as he spoke and extracted a piece of paper. 'As it happens,' he went on, 'I have the proposal form with me here, already filled in. All that you would need to do is to sign it. Thank you so much for doing this.'

Von Igelfeld looked about him. Señor Gabriel Marcales de Cinco Fermentaciones had placed him in an acutely embarrassing position. If he turned him down, it would be an act of gross ingratitude to the man who, presumably, had arranged his own nomination as Corresponding Fellow. And yet, if he proposed him, the President and Members could be placed in a situation where they would be obliged to elect somebody whom, for all von Igelfeld knew, they may not have wished to elect in the first place.

'This is where you sign,' said Cinco Fermentaciones, placing the paper, and a pen, in von Igelfeld's hands.

There was really no alternative, and so von Igelfeld signed, handing the paper back to Cinco Fermentaciones with an angry glance. This glance either went unnoticed, or was ignored.

'You are very kind,' said Cinco Fermentaciones. 'Now I am in,' adding, 'at last.' He leant forward and embraced von Igelfeld, muttering further words of gratitude as he did so.

Von Igelfeld bore the embrace and the words of thanks with fortitude. He had walked right into a South American trap, and perhaps he should have realised it earlier. But the important thing was that whatever the motive of Cinco Fermentaciones had been in proposing him, the fact remained that he was now a Corresponding Fellow of the Academy of Letters of Colombia, an honour which had eluded even Zimmermann. And even if the President of the Academy were to be annoyed with him for proposing Cinco Fermentaciones, he would probably never encounter the President in the future and thus there would be few occasions for awkwardness.

Cinco Fermentaciones beamed with satisfaction. 'Now,' he said, 'we – or, rather I, have planned a few days for you in the country, as a reward, so to speak, for your having come all this way. A very well-known lady, who has perhaps the finest literary salon in all South America, has specially invited us to her villa in the hills. It will be a real treat.'

'I am most grateful,' said von Igelfeld. A few days in the country, being well looked after, would suit him very well. He was not due back in Germany for over a week, and what could be more enjoyable than sitting on a shady verandah, listening to the sounds of flocks of tropical birds, and knowing that at the end of the day a fine meal awaited one.

They returned to the hotel, where von Igelfeld packed his bags and had them carried to the car which Cinco Fermentaciones provided. Then, after a fortifying cup of coffee, they set off down a pot-holed road, through sprawling crowded suburbs, into the countryside. The warmth of the car and the drone of the engine made von Igelfeld feel drowsy, and by the time he woke up, they were driving down what appeared to be a private road, through plantations of fruit trees, towards a large, ochre-coloured house on the lower slopes of a mountain.

'The home of Señora Dolores Quinta Barranquilla,' said Cinco Fermentaciones. 'Our journey is at an end. We have arrived at the Villa of Reduced Circumstances.'

A servant met them at the large front door of the villa. He was a small man in an ill-fitting black jacket and wearing grubby white gloves. He took the suitcases from the back of the car and gestured for Cinco Fermentaciones and von Igelfeld to follow him. They went inside, into a house of high-ceilinged cool rooms, furnished with dark mahogany chairs and tables in the Spanish colonial style, with painted cupboards on which fruits, Virgins and hunting

dogs competed for space with pink-faced cherubs. Then they passed through a portico into a courtyard, around the sides of which were arranged the doors which gave on to their respective bedrooms.

Left by himself in his bedroom, von Igelfeld unpacked his suitcase and noticed, with satisfaction, a spacious writing desk on which supplies of paper, along with bottles of ink and a stick pen, had been laid. To the right of the desk was a bookcase housing several shelves of books. He glanced at the titles: there were collected essays, novels, works of philosophy, and several volumes of the poems of Pablo Neruda. He picked up one of the Neruda volumes, noting an inscription on the fly leaf: *Quinta Barranquilla, from his life-long friend, Pablo Neruda: I am not worthy of your friendship, but I have it nonetheless, and am content.* Von Igelfeld was intrigued; the salon run by Dolores Quinta Barranquilla was clearly every bit as distinguished as Cinco Fermentaciones had implied. He replaced the book and picked up the volume next to it, a Spanish translation of Hemingway. Von Igelfeld was not impressed by Hemingway, whom he had never read and whom he had no intention of reading. In his view, those who practised hunting and fighting in wars should not write books, as there was nothing of any interest to literature in those pursuits. Hemingway was a fine example of this. No German writer would have gone bull-fighting in Spain or deep-sea fishing off Cuba, and this showed in the almost total absence of these themes in German literature. He placed the Hemingway back on the shelf with distaste and looked out of the window. In the middle of the courtyard there was a small fountain, out of which water played gently. On a stone bench beside the fountain sat Cinco Fermentaciones, and at his side, engaged in earnest conversation with him, was a middle-aged woman in a red skirt and white blouse. This, von Igelfeld assumed, was Dolores Quinta Barranquilla. He moved closer to the window and stared at her, struck by her peaceful expression. It was a Madonna-like face of the sort that is not all that unusual in the Latin world; a face which Botticelli or Mantegna might have painted. He gazed at her, and as he did so, she suddenly looked up and met his eyes. Von Igelfeld froze, unable to move away from the window, but mortified to be caught in the act of spying upon his hostess. Then the spell broke, and he withdrew from the window, back into the shadows of his room.

A few minutes later, when he heard the knock on the door, he imagined that it was Dolores Quinta Barranquilla, and that she was coming to ask him to explain himself. He answered with some trepidation, but found that it was only the manservant in his ill-fitting jacket, who announced that drinks would be served in the salon at seven o'clock that evening and that the Señora would be honoured by Professor von Igelfeld's presence at that time. Von Igelfeld thanked him and the manservant nodded. If His Excellency was in need of anything, he was only to ring the bell which he would find in his room; they were short-staffed, alas! as things were not quite what they were in the past, but they would do their best.

'We are deeply honoured, Professor von Igelfeld,' said Dolores Quinta Barranquilla. 'Is that not so, Gabriel?'

'Indeed it is,' said Cinco Fermentaciones.

'To have a Fellow of the Academy of Letters in the house is always rewarding,' went on Dolores Quinta Barranquilla, 'but to have a Corresponding Fellow, why, that's a very particular distinction! Indeed, I cannot remember when last that happened.'

'Five years ago,' offered Cinco Fermentaciones.

Dolores Quinta Barranquilla thanked him for the information. 'Five long years!' she said. 'Five arid years now ended!'

Cinco Fermentaciones smiled. 'Indeed, this evening is almost like a meeting of the Academy.'

Dolores Quinta Barranquilla looked at him blankly, and he continued: 'You see, my dear Señora Dolores, we almost have two Members of the Academy in the room. I myself . . . '

Dolores Quinta Barranquilla clasped her hands together in delight. ' . . . have been elected! I am thrilled, Gabriel. At last those provincial fools have begun to understand . . . '

'Not quite,' said Cinco Fermentaciones quickly. 'Please note that I said *almost* two Members. I have been nominated. Indeed, my nomination is quite recent, but I have every reason to believe that it will lead to my election to the Academy.'

Dolores Quinta Barranquilla turned to von Igelfeld and fixed him with a warm smile. 'I suspect that we might have you to thank for this,' she said. 'Our dear friend Gabriel has not been given the recognition that he deserves, I'm afraid. It comes from being out of Colombia.'

Cinco Fermentaciones held up a hand to protest. 'You are too kind, Señora Dolores. My contribution is small.'

'It was an honour to be able to propose Señor Gabriel Marcales de Cinco Fermentaciones,' contributed von Igelfeld. 'His work in . . . ' he paused, and there was an awkward silence as they both turned to look at him. Von Igelfeld was quite unaware of his candidate's work. Had Cinco Fermentaciones written a book? Possibly, but if he had, then he had no means of telling what it was and whether it was good or bad. Of course, one did not become a cultural attaché for nothing, and he must have done something, possibly more than enough to deserve membership of the Academy of Letters. He took a deep breath. 'His work in all respects is well-known.'

Dolores Quinta Barranquilla raised an eyebrow. 'There are those who say that he bought the job,' she said, going on quickly. 'But I hasten to say that I am most certainly not one of those! There are so many people in this country who are consumed by envy. There are even some who say that I bought this villa, would you believe it?'

'And you did not?' asked von Igelfeld.

'Certainly not,' replied Dolores Quinta Barranquilla. 'Everything you see about you belonged to my paternal grandfather, Don Alfonso Quinta Barranquilla. I have bought nothing – nothing at all.'

'The Señora is modest,' said Cinco Fermentaciones unctuously. 'Even in her grandfather's day, the villa was the centre of intellectual life in Colombia. Everybody of any note came out from the capital at weekends and participated in the discussion that took place in this very room. Everybody. And then, more recently, in the days of her father, Neruda began to call when he was in this country. He would spend weeks here. He wrote many poems in this very room.'

'I am a great admirer of his work,' said von Igelfeld. 'His Spanish is very fine.'

'He is still with us, I feel,' said Dolores Quinta Barranquilla dreamily. 'Do you not feel that, Gabriel? Do you not feel Pablo's presence?'

'I do,' said Cinco Fermentaciones. 'I feel that he is with us here at the moment.'

'As are all the others,' went on Dolores Quinta Barranquilla. 'Marquez. Valderrama. Pessoa. Yes, Pessoa, dear Professor von Igelfeld. He travelled up from Brazil and spent several weeks in this house, in the time of my father. They talked and talked, he told me. My father, like you, was fluent in Portuguese. He and Pessoa sat here, in this very room, and talked the night away.'

Von Igelfeld looked about the room. He could imagine Pessoa sitting here, with his large hat on the table by the window, or on his knee perhaps; really, these were most agreeable surroundings, and the hostess, too, was utterly charming, with her mellifluous voice and her sympathetic understanding of literature. He could talk the night away, he felt, and perhaps they would.

The conversation continued in this pleasant way for an hour or so before they moved through for dinner. This was served in an adjoining room, by a middle-aged cook in an apron. Von Igelfeld had expected generous fare, but the portions were small and the wine was thin. The conversation, of course, more than made up for this, but he found himself reflecting on the name of the villa and the parsimony of the table. These thoughts distressed him: there was something inexpressibly sad about faded grandeur. There may well have been a salon in this house, and it may well have been a distinguished one, but what was left now? Only memories, it would seem.

Von Igelfeld slept soundly. It had been an exhilarating evening, and he had listened attentively to his hostess's observations on a wide range of topics. All of these observations had struck him as being both perceptive and sound, which made the evening one of rare agreement. Now, standing at his window the following morning, he looked out on to the courtyard with its small fountain, its stone bench, and its display of brilliant flowering shrubs. It was a magnificent morning and von Igelfeld decided that he would take a brief walk about the fruit groves before breakfast was served.

Donning his newly acquired Panama hat, he walked through the courtyard and made his way towards the front door. It was at this point, as he walked through one of the salons, that he noticed a number of rather ill-kempt men standing about. They looked at him suspiciously and did not respond when von Igelfeld politely said, 'Buenos Dias.' Perhaps they were the estate workers, thought von Igelfeld, and they were simply taciturn. When he reached the font door, however, a man moved out in front of him and blocked his way.

'Who are you?' the man asked roughly.

Von Igelfeld looked at the man before him. He was wearing dark breeches, a red shirt, and was unshaven. His manner could only be described as insolent, and von Igelfeld decided that much as one did not like to complain to one's hostess, this was a case which might merit a complaint. Who was he indeed! He was the author of *Portuguese Irregular Verbs*, that's who he was, and he was minded to tell this man just that. But instead he merely said: 'I am Professor Dr Moritz-Maria von Igelfeld. That's who I am. And who are you?'

The man, who had been leaning against the jamb of the door, now straightened up and approached von Igelfeld threateningly. 'I? I?' he said, his tone unambiguously hostile. 'I am Pedro. That's who I am. Pedro, leader of Movimiento Veintitrés.'

'Movimiento Veintitrés?' said von Igelfeld, trying to sound confident, but suddenly feeling somewhat concerned. He remembered the warnings uttered by Cinco Fermentaciones in the hotel in Bogotá. Had Movimiento Veintitrés featured in the list of those who were dangerous? He could not remember, but as he looked at Pedro, standing there with his hands in the pockets of his black breeches and his eyes glinting dangerously, he thought that perhaps it had.

Von Igelfeld swallowed. 'How do you do, Señor Pedro,' he said.

Pedro did not respond to the greeting. After a while, however, he turned his head to one side and spat on the floor.

'Oh,' said von Igelfeld. 'I hope that you are in good health.'

Pedro spat again. 'We have taken over this house and this land,' said Pedro. 'You are now a captive of the people of Colombia, as are the so-called Señora Barranquilla and Señor Gabriel. You will all be subject to the revolutionary justice of Movimiento Veintitrés.'

Von Igelfeld stood stock still. 'I am a prisoner?' he stuttered. 'I?'

Pedro nodded. 'You are under arrest. But you will be given a fair trial before you are shot. I can give you my word as to that.'

Von Igelfeld stared at Pedro. Perhaps he had misheard. Perhaps this was an elaborate practical joke; in which case it was in extremely poor taste. 'Hah!' he said, trying to smile. 'That is very amusing. Very amusing.'

'No, it isn't,' said Pedro. 'It is not amusing at all. It is very sad . . . for you, that is.'

'But I am a visitor,' said von Igelfeld. 'I have nothing to do with whatever is going on. I don't even know what you are talking about.'

'Then you'll find out soon enough,' said Pedro. 'In the meantime, you must join the others. They are in that room over there. They will explain the situation to you.'

Von Igelfeld moved over towards the door pointed out by Pedro.

'Go on,' said Pedro, taunting him. 'They are in there. You go and join them, Señor German. Your pampered friends are in there. They are expecting you.'

Von Igelfeld entered the room. Sitting on a sofa in the middle of the floor were Señora Dolores Quinta Barranquilla and Cinco Fermentaciones. As he opened the door, they looked up expectantly.

'Señor Gabriel Marcales de Cinco Fermentaciones,' said von Igelfeld, 'what is the meaning of all this, may I ask you? Will you kindly explain?'

Cinco Fermentaciones sighed. 'We have fallen into the hands of guerrillas,' he said. 'That is what's happened.'

'It's the end for us,' added Dolores Quinta Barranquilla, shaking her head miserably. 'Movimiento Veintitrés! The very worst.'

'The worst of the worst,' said Cinco Fermentaciones. 'I'm afraid that there is no hope. No hope at all.'

Von Igelfeld stood quite still. He had taken in what his friends had said, but he found it difficult to believe what he was hearing. This sort of thing – falling into the hands of guerrillas – was not something that happened to professors of philology, and yet Pedro was real enough, as was the fear that he appeared to have engendered in his hosts. Oh, if only he had been wise enough not to come! This is what happened to one when one went off in pursuit of honours; Nemesis, ever vigilant, was looking out for hubris, and he had given her a fine target indeed. Now it was too late. They would all be shot – or so Pedro seemed to assume – and that would be the end of everything. For a moment he imagined the others at coffee on the day on which the news came through. The Librarian would be tearful, Prinzel would be silenced with grief, and Unterholzer . . . Unterholzer would regret him, no doubt, but would even then be planning to move into his room on a permanent basis. Was that not exactly what had happened when he had been thought to have been lost at sea?

Von Igelfeld's thoughts were interrupted by Dolores Quinta Barranquilla. 'I am truly sorry, Professor von Igelfeld,' she said. 'This is no way for a country to treat a distinguished visitor. Shooting a visitor is the height, the absolute height, of impoliteness.'

'Certainly it is,' agreed Cinco Fermentaciones. 'This is a matter of the greatest possible regret to me too.'

Von Igelfeld thanked them for their concern. 'Perhaps they will change their minds,' he said. 'We might even be rescued.'

'No chance of that,' said Cinco Fermentaciones. 'The Army is pretty useless and, anyway, they probably have no idea that the place has been taken by these . . . these desperadoes.' He looked up as he uttered this last phrase. Pedro had appeared at the door and was looking in, relishing the discomfort of his prisoners.

'You may move around if you wish,' he said. 'You may enjoy the open air. The sky. The sound of the birds singing. Enjoy them and reflect on them while you may.' He laughed, and moved away.

'What a cruel and unpleasant man,' said von Igelfeld.

'They are all like that,' sighed Cinco Fermentaciones. 'They have no heart.'

Dolores Quinta Barranquilla seemed lost in thought. 'Not everyone can be entirely bad,' she said. 'Even the entirely bad.'

Von Igelfeld and Cinco Fermentaciones stared at her uncomprehendingly, but she seemed in no mood to explain her puzzling utterance. Rising to her feet, she announced that she would go for a walk, would do some sketching, and looked forward to seeing them both at dinner.

Von Igelfeld was aware of a great deal of coming and going among the guerrillas during the course of the day, but paid them little attention. He went for a brief walk in the late morning, but found the constant tailing presence of a young guerrilla disconcerting and he returned to the villa after ten minutes or so. It seemed that although Pedro was prepared to allow them to wander about the villa, he was determined that they should not escape.

After an afternoon of reading in his room, von Igelfeld dressed carefully for dinner. Whatever the uncertain future held, and however truncated that future might be, he was not prepared to allow his personal standards to slip. Dressed in the smart white suit which he had brought on the trip he crossed the courtyard and made his way into the salon where Cinco Fermentaciones and Dolores Quinta Barranquilla were already sipping glasses of wine. They were not the only ones present, however: Pedro, dressed now in a black jacket, a pair of smartly pressed red trousers, and a pair of highly polished knee-high boots was standing with them, glass of wine in hand, engaged in conversation.

'That's very interesting,' he said, referring to a point which Dolores Quinta Barranquilla had made just before von Igelfeld's entry into the room. 'Do you mean to say that Adolfo Bioy Casares himself was here. In this very room?'

'Absolutely,' replied Dolores Quinta Barranquilla. 'He spent many hours talking to my father. I was a young girl, of course, but I remember him well. He wrote us long letters from Buenos Aires. I used to write to him and ask him about his first novel, *Iris y Margarita*.'

'Remarkable,' said Pedro.

'I remember telling Che about that,' Dolores Quinta Barranquilla went on. 'He was very intrigued.'

Pedro gave a start. 'Che?'

'Guevara,' Dolores Quinta Barranquilla said smoothly. 'Che Guevara. He called on a number of occasions. Discreetly, of course. But my father and I always got on so well with him. I miss him terribly.'

'He was in this house?' said Pedro.

'Of course,' said Dolores Quinta Barranquilla. 'Such a nice man.'

Pedro nodded. 'He is sorely missed.'

'But now we have you!' said Dolores Quinta Barranquilla. 'Perhaps one day you'll be as well-known as dear Che. Who knows.'

Pedro smiled modestly and took a sip of his wine. 'I don't think so.'

'You're too modest,' said von Igelfeld. 'You never know. I used to be unknown. Now I am a bit better known.'

'That is true,' said Cinco Fermentaciones. 'And now Professor von Igelfeld has become a Corresponding Fellow of the Academy of Letters.'

'Really?' exclaimed Pedro. 'Well, my congratulations on that.' He looked at von Igelfeld, as if with new eyes. 'You don't think . . . ' he began. 'Might it be possible . . . '

Von Igelfeld did not require any more pressing. 'I would be

honoured to propose you as a Member of the Academy. I should be delighted, in fact.'

'And I would support your nomination,' chipped in Cinco Fermentaciones. 'I am virtually a Member myself and could expect to become a full Member provided . . . provided I survive.'

'But of course you'll survive,' laughed Pedro. 'Whatever made you think to the contrary?'

'Something you said,' muttered Cinco Fermentaciones. 'I thought that . . . '

'Oh that,' said Pedro nonchalantly. 'I'm always threatening to shoot people. Pay no attention to that.'

'You mean you never carry out your threats?' asked von Igelfeld.

Pedro looked slightly uncomfortable. 'Sometimes,' he said. 'It depends on whether it's historically necessary to shoot somebody. In your case, it is no longer historically necessary to shoot you.'

'I am pleased to hear that,' said von Igelfeld.

'Good,' said Dolores Quinta Barranquilla. 'Well, that's settled then. Let's go through for dinner. After you, Pedrissimo!'

Pedro laughed. 'That is a good name. My men would respect me more if I were called Pedrissimo. That is an excellent suggestion on your part.'

'I am always pleased to help Movimiento Veintidós,' said Dolores Quinta Barranquilla.

'Movimiento Veintitrés,' corrected Pedro, almost pedantically, thought von Igelfeld; or certainly with a greater degree of pedantry than one would expect of a guerrilla leader.

'Precisely,' said Dolores Quinta Barranquilla, taking her place at the head of the table. 'Now, Professor von Igelfeld, you sit there, and Gabriel, you sit over there. And this seat here, on my right, is reserved for you, dear Pedrissimo.'

Dolores Quinta Barranquilla had instructed the kitchen to make a special effort, and they had risen to the challenge. The depths of the cellar had been plumbed for the few remaining great wines (laid down some twenty years earlier by Don Quinta Barranquilla, who might not have imagined the company which would eventually consume them). These were served directly from the bottle, as decanting would have caused such vintages to fade. They were particularly appreciated by Pedro, who became more and more agreeable as the evening wore on. It might be impossible for him to travel to Bogotá in the near future to receive his Academy Membership, owing to the fact that the Government had put a price on his head ('Such provincial dolts,' Dolores Quinta Barranquilla had observed); however, he would be able to do so he hoped in the future, under a more equitable constitution.

They ended the evening with toasts. Pedro toasted von Igelfeld, and expressed the hope that the rest of his stay in Colombia would be a pleasant one; Dolores Quinta Barranquilla proposed a toast to Pedro, and hoped that he would shortly be received into the Academy; and Cinco Fermentaciones proposed a toast to the imminent success of Movimiento Veintidós, rapidly correcting this to Veintitrés on a glance from Dolores Quinta Barranquilla. Finally, von Igelfeld gave a brief recital of *Auf ein altes Bild* by Mörike, which Pedro asked him to write down and translate into Spanish when he had the time to do so.

Replete after the excellent meal, they all retired to bed and slept soundly until the next morning, when, to von Igelfeld's alarm, they were awakened by the sound of gunfire. Von Igelfeld tumbled out of bed, donned his dressing-gown, and peered out of the window. A group of thirty or forty of Pedro's men were marshalled in the courtyard, breaking open a crate of weapons and handing them round. Dolores Quinta Barranquilla was there too, helping to pass guns to the guerrillas. Von Igelfeld gasped. They had got on extremely well with Pedro the previous evening, and both sides had obviously reassessed their view of one another, but he had not imagined that it would lead to their all effectively joining Pedro in his struggle. And yet there was Dolores Quinta Barranquilla, rolling up her sleeves and organising the guerrillas, and was that not Cinco Fermentaciones himself perched on the roof, rifle at the ready?

Von Igelfeld dressed and waited in his room. A few minutes later, there was a knock on his door and he opened it to find Dolores Quinta Barranquilla standing there, a rifle in her right hand and another in her left.

'Here's yours,' she said, handing him the rifle. 'The ammunition is over there.'

Von Igelfeld could not conceal his astonishment. 'I don't want this,' he said, thrusting the rifle back at her.

Dolores Quinta Barranquilla looked over her shoulder. 'You have to take it,' she whispered. 'If you don't, he'll shoot you. And if he doesn't shoot you, then the Army will shoot you if they take this place from the guerrillas. The local Army commander has a terrible reputation for not taking prisoners. So you effectively have no choice.' She pushed the rifle back into von Igelfeld's hands and gestured for him to follow her.

'I'll find a position where you won't be in danger,' she said. 'You can go to my study window. It's very small and it gives a good view of the driveway. If the Army comes up the driveway, you'll have plenty of time to pick them off without being too exposed yourself. It's the best place to defend the villa without too much personal risk.'

Mutely, von Igelfeld followed her to his allotted position and crouched down beside her window.

'You see,' said Dolores Quinta Barranquilla. 'That gives you a clear field of fire. Have you ever fired a rifle before?'

'Certainly not,' said von Igelfeld. 'The very idea.'

'Oh dear,' said Dolores Quinta Barranquilla. 'Well, you just look down those sights there and try to line them up against an Army target. Then you pull that thing there – that's a trigger. That's the way it works.'

Von Igelfeld nodded miserably. The pleasure at last night's reprieve was now completely destroyed. He couldn't possibly fire at the Army if they came down the driveway, but then what should he do? There was always the possibility of surrender, once the Army approached the house. Perhaps he could tie a piece of white cloth to the end of his rifle and stick that out of the window, but then that would hardly be effective if Pedro's men continued to fire from their positions. It was all very vexing.

Dolores Quinta Barranquilla left him in her study and went off to busy herself with passing ammunition to the guerrillas in their various positions about the house. Von Igelfeld drew a chair up to the window and sat down. He looked out down the driveway, along the line of trees that formed an avenue approaching the villa, to the countryside beyond. It all looked so peaceful, and yet even as he contemplated the scene there would be soldiers scuttling about in the undergrowth, edging their way into firing positions, ready to storm the villa. The sound of firing which he had heard earlier on had now died away, and there was a strange, almost preternatural quiet, as if Nature herself were holding her breath.

Von Igelfeld thought about his life and what he had done with it. He had done his best, he reflected, even if there was much that he still wished to accomplish. If the day turned out in the way in which he thought it might, then at least he had left something behind him. He had left *Portuguese Irregular Verbs*, all twelve hundred pages of it, and that was an achievement. It was certainly more than Unterholzer had done . . . but, no, he checked himself. That was not an appropriate line of thought to pursue. He should not leave this world with uncharitable thoughts in his mind; rather, he should spend his last few hours – or even minutes – thinking thoughts which were worthy of the author of *Portuguese Irregular Verbs*. These were . . . Now that he tried to identify them, no worthy thoughts came.

A shot rang out, and von Igelfeld grabbed his rifle, which had been resting against Dolores Quinta Barranquilla's desk. He looked out of the window. There was a small cloud of smoke over the orchard, and then, quite loud enough to rattle the glass in the study windows, there came the sound of an explosion. A man shouted – something unintelligible – and then the quiet returned.

Very slowly, von Igelfeld edged up the sash window and began to stick the end of the rifle outside. He paused. This brave gesture had produced no result. He was still there, alive, and nothing outside seemed to stir. This is war, he thought; this is the confusion of the battlefield. It is all so peaceful.

He looked down the avenue of trees. Was that a movement? He strained his eyes to see, trying to decide whether a shape underneath an orange tree was a person, a sack, or a mound of earth. He pointed the gun at it and looked down the sights. There was a V and a small protuberance of metal at the end of the barrel. Dolores Quinta Barranquilla had told him how to fire the weapon, but now that he was faced with the need to do so, he could not remember exactly what it was that he was meant to do. His finger reached for the trigger, fumbled slightly with the guard that surrounded it, and then found its position.

Von Igelfeld pulled the trigger. There was a loud report, which made him reel backwards, away from the window, and from the outside there came a shout. He closed his eyes, and then opened them again, his heart thudding within his chest. He had apparently fired the rifle and something had happened outside. Had he shot somebody? The thought appalled him. He had not the slightest desire to harm anybody, even the Colombian Army. It was a terrible thing to do; to come to a country to receive the Corresponding Fellowship of its Academy of Letters and then to open fire on the Army. Mind you, he reflected, he had not asked to come to the Villa of Reduced Circumstances; he had not asked to be kidnapped by guerrillas; and he had certainly not asked to be placed at this window with this rifle in his hands.

There was more shouting outside, and this was greeted by shouts from the villa itself. After a moment, there was silence, and then another shout. And then, to von Igelfeld's astonishment, a man emerged from behind a tree, a mere two hundred yards from the villa, and put his hands up. He turned round and shouted something, and suddenly a whole crowd appeared from the orchard and the surrounding trees, all of them shouting, lighting cigarettes and, in some cases, throwing weapons to the ground. The man who had come out first continued to shout at them and was now approaching the villa. As he did so, Pedro came out of the front door and walked briskly across to meet him. The two shook hands, and then Pedro slapped the other man on the back and they began to walk back towards the front of the house. As he neared the door, Pedro turned in the direction of von Igelfeld's window and gave him a cheerful wave, accompanied by an encouraging gesture of some sort.

'Comrades!' shouted Pedro to the large group of guerrillas who had gathered in the courtyard, drinking red wine from paper cups. 'We have secured a great victory. The Provincial Army Headquarters this morning surrendered the entire province to our control. You saw it happen. You saw the Colonel here get up and surrender. Wise man! Now he is with us, fighting alongside us, and brings all his armoured cars and helicopters with him.'

These words were greeted with a loud cheering, and several paper cups were tossed into the air in celebration. Pedro, standing on a chair, smiled at his men.

'And there is one man who brought this about,' he declaimed. 'There is one man who – myself excepted, of course – deserves more credit than anybody else for this great victory. This is the man who fired the shot that tipped the balance and brought the Army to its senses. That man, comrades in arms, is standing right over there in the shadows. That man is Professor el Coronel von Igelfeld!'

For a moment von Igelfeld was too stunned to do or say anything. But he did not need to, as the guerrillas had turned round and were looking at him as he stood on the small verandah outside Dolores Quinta Barranquilla's study.

'Well,' he said at last. 'I'm not sure . . . I was sitting there and I suppose that . . . '

His words were heard by nobody, as the guerrillas, now joined by another fifty or sixty men in the uniform of the Colombian Army, began to roar their approval.

'*Viva!*' they shouted. '*Viva el Coronel von Igelfeld! Viva!*'

Von Igelfeld blushed. This was most extraordinary behaviour on their part, but then they were Colombians, after all, and South Americans had a tendency to be excitable. As the cries of *Viva!* echoed about the courtyard, he raised a hand hesitantly and waved at the men. This brought further cheers and cries.

'*Viva Pedrissimo!*' shouted von Igelfeld at last. '*Viva el Movimiento! Viva el pueblo Colombiano!*'

These were very appropriate sentiments, and the words were well-chosen. The guerrillas, who had now consumed more wine, were encouraged to shout out further complimentary remarks, and von Igelfeld waved again, more confidently this time. Then he returned to the study, the cries of *Viva!* ringing in his ears. He had noticed a very interesting book on Dolores Quinta Barranquilla's shelves, and he intended to read it while Pedro and his new-found friends got on with the business of the revolution. Really, it was all very tedious and he had had quite enough of military action. It had been very satisfactory being applauded by the guerrillas in that way, but the satisfaction was a hollow one, he thought, and was certainly much less rewarding than being elected a Corresponding Fellow of the Academy.

Von Igelfeld sat in the study until lunch time, reading the book he had discovered. There was a great deal of bustle about the villa, and several armoured cars and trucks arrived outside during the course of the morning. He thought of complaining to Pedro about the noise, as it was very difficult to read while all this was going on, but he eventually decided that he was a guest at this particular revolution and it would be rude to complain about the noise which his hosts were making. He would not have hesitated to do so in comparable circumstances in Germany, but in Colombia one had to make allowances.

Shortly before lunch was served, a helicopter arrived. Von Igelfeld watched it with annoyance from his window. Was it an Italian helicopter, he wondered, made in Count Augusta's helicopter factory near Bologna? He would ask at lunch, not that he expected to find anybody who knew anything about it, but he could ask. Several men in uniform stepped out of the helicopter and there were further cries of *Viva!* and even more bustle. Von Igelfeld returned to his book.

He was called to lunch by Dolores Quinta Barranquilla. He had not seen much of her during the morning, and she now appeared in a fresh outfit, a fetching red bandana tied about her neck and secured with a large emerald pin.

'I do hope that you're not too bored,' she said airily. 'Pedro and

I have been very busy indeed. That was a General arriving in that helicopter. He says that the capital is falling – useless provincials – and that the Government is on the point of capitulation to the Movimiento. It's all happened before, of course, and it doesn't make much difference in the long run.'

'But I thought you said they were ruthless guerrillas,' said von Igelfeld, inserting a bookmark in the book. 'You implied that they were worse than anybody else. I heard you. You said that. You did.'

Dolores Quinta Barranquilla shrugged. 'Circumstances change. Look at Pedro himself. He's really rather well-educated. He knows how to behave. I see no reason why he shouldn't be in the Government. Nobody can run this country, so it may as well be Pedro and his friends who don't run it.'

Von Igelfeld thought about this for a moment. 'I was wondering about leaving, Señora Dolores Quinta Barranquilla,' he said. 'I must say that I've enjoyed being at the villa, but I do have to return home, you know.'

'But of course,' said Dolores Quinta Barranquilla. 'There will be no problem over that. Of course we shall miss you, dear Professor von Igelfeld. I'll speak to Pedro. Perhaps you can go back to Bogotá in the helicopter, once the city has finally fallen. I don't expect you'll have to wait all that long.'

'That would be very satisfactory,' said von Igelfeld. 'I think I have had enough history for one day.'

'I shall talk to dear Pedro about it,' said Dolores Quinta Barranquilla. 'He's very reasonable, you know. All he wants to do is to help. There are men like that, you know. Not many, of course. But they do exist.'

The kitchen, which had excelled itself the previous night, again rose to the occasion. Further dusty bottles of wine were located in the cellar, and the cook, who was the elder brother of the manservant, retrieved his finest ingredients from the larder, including porcini mushrooms that had been preserved since the days of Dolores Quinta Barranquilla's father and were approaching their peak of flavour, pickled beans, and dried fish from Cartagena. Von Igelfeld was hungry from the morning's exertions, and thoroughly agreed with the observation made by Cinco Fermentaciones that battle sharpened the appetite. He made a mental note to mention this in a letter to Zimmermann, who would not be in a position to contradict the proposition and would undoubtedly be very impressed. Indeed, there were few people in von Igelfeld's circle who would be able to make such a comment, a thought which gave von Igelfeld some satisfaction.

There were two extra guests at the lunch table. Von Igelfeld sat next to the Colonel who had surrendered, a charming man, he thought, who had a strong interest in the history of the Jesuits in South America. Then, on the other side of the table, was the General who had arrived by helicopter. He was a large man in a bottle-green uniform on which numerous military decorations had been pinned. He appeared distrustful of Pedro at first, but after the first course they became involved in a protracted political debate which seemed to bring them closer together. The General drank more wine than was necessary, thought von Igelfeld, and he hoped that he would not be at the controls of the helicopter if they were to go back to Bogotá that afternoon.

The Colonel had been informed of von Igelfeld's central role in that morning's encounter, and was full of praise for his courage and accuracy with a rifle.

'I realised immediately that the odds were unequal,' he said. 'That shot you fired went straight through the peak of my cap, just like that. I knew that if you could place a bullet so accurately, we would have little chance.'

'I am glad that we avoided bloodshed,' said von Igelfeld modestly.

'I only wish that our own professors were so brave,' remarked the Colonel. 'I cannot imagine that they would be much good. But then, I suppose you haven't met many of them.'

'Oh, I have met them,' said von Igelfeld. 'There were a number at a meeting of the Academy of Letters which I recently attended.'

The Colonel put down his knife and fork and turned towards von Igelfeld. 'The Academy? In Bogotá? You're a Member?'

'I am a Corresponding Fellow,' said von Igelfeld. 'I have only been to one meeting so far.'

The Colonel looked thoughtful. 'As a Corresponding Fellow,' he began, 'would you be entitled to propose new Members, I wonder? Would you be entitled, do you think?'

Von Igelfeld looked down at his plate. He was becoming used to South American ways and perhaps there was no point in protesting. If this was the way in which the country worked, then he should perhaps accept it. No one person can change the *mores* of an entire nation.

'I should be pleased to propose you, Colonel,' he said. 'I am sure that your scholarship merits it.'

'Oh, thank you! Thank you!' enthused the Colonel. 'The Academy! Thank you so much.'

'Not at all,' said von Igelfeld. 'We can pick up the proposal papers when we get back to Bogotá. Then I shall sign them immediately.'

'You're an excellent man,' said the Colonel. 'Now would you like a further glass of wine? I must say that the Señora keeps a wonderful cellar, doesn't she?'

Their conversation was interrupted by Pedro, who rose to his feet, glass in hand. One of his men had slipped into the room and had whispered a message. Pedro, having dismissed him, made a sign to the General, who nodded.

'Señora, Gentlemen,' began Pedro in formal tones. 'I have this minute heard from my intelligence officer. The Government in Bogotá is no more. The President of the Republic has decamped to Miami and the instruments of Government have been placed in the hands of our Movement. The way is clear for us to return to the capital and assume our rightful place in government. I now ask you to join me in drinking the health of the new Government!'

They all rose. 'To the Government!' said the General in a loud voice. 'To the Government and *la Patria*!'

'And to our dear Pedrissimo!' added Dolores Quinta Barranquilla. 'How fortunate that day – only yesterday, I believe – that you joined us at the Villa of Reduced Circumstances!'

'Thank you,' said Pedro, 'my dear friends. We have great works ahead of us, believe me. But we shall accomplish these with alacrity and take the country forward into a new age of prosperity and achievement. That is what I believe. That is the policy of the new Government.'

'A very fine philosophy,' whispered the Colonel to von Igelfeld. 'Exactly the same philosophy as that professed by the last Government, and the Government before it.'

'And did they achieve what they set out to achieve?' asked von Igelfeld.

'Good heavens, no,' said the Colonel. 'But then governments

don't run this country. This country is run by *narcotraficantes* and the like. Governments are window-dressing in this part of the world.'

'I find that very hard to believe,' said von Igelfeld. 'Surely you could not have a country run by criminals. Surely that is impossible.'

'*Au contraire*,' said the Colonel, reaching for a tooth-pick. 'That is exactly what happens. And our friend Pedro and his cronies know it full well. Just wait and see. Just you wait and see.'

They were told at the end of lunch to prepare themselves for departure to Bogotá. Dolores Quinta Barranquilla had decided to stay behind, in spite of being invited to go to Bogotá and join the new Government. She had a responsibility for the villa, she explained, but she would like to have them all out for a literary weekend – the entire Cabinet – as soon as possible. Pedro thought this a good idea and got out his diary to check dates. So with Dolores Quinta Barranquilla staying behind, Cinco Fermentaciones, von Igelfeld, Pedro, the General and the Colonel would all fly down to Bogotá in the General's helicopter.

Von Igelfeld packed his suitcase and made his way out to the helicopter. Climbing in, he noticed, to his relief, that the General was not proposing to pilot the aircraft, but that a moustachioed pilot in dark glasses was seated at the controls. Soon they were all strapped into their seats and with a great whirring of blades the helicopter pulled itself up into the mid-afternoon air. Down below, holding on to her hat in the breeze from the rotors, Dolores Quinta Barranquilla looked up and waved. Von Igelfeld waved back. She had been a fine hostess, and a brave one too. They would meet again, he hoped, perhaps in the not-too-distant future. And it was then that the thought occurred. *You should marry her.* He smiled. Impossible. *No, it would not be.*

They hovered over the villa for a moment, as if acknowledging the cheers of the guerrillas and soldiers down below. Then, swooping off, away from the mountainside behind the villa, they set off for Bogotá and for the political destiny that awaited them. Von Igelfeld closed his eyes. Soon he would be back in Germany, back in the Institute. He would be talking to Herr Huber over coffee. He would be inspecting his room for signs of intrusion by Unterholzer. He would be passing on *Zeitschrift* articles to Prinzel for checking. South America, and its revolutions, would be many miles away, a dim memory of a life which he had glimpsed and which had embraced him so wholeheartedly in its contortions. On balance he was glad that all this had happened, though, that he had been a man of action and come through it, alive. Now there was even less reason to read Hemingway. It would all seem too tame, too unrealistic.

Von Igelfeld spent that night in Cinco Fermentaciones' house in the centre of Bogotá. It was a noisy evening, as the population was out in full strength to celebrate the new Government. Fireworks were exploded and there was singing, but von Igelfeld succeeded nonetheless in sleeping well. The following morning, over break-fast, he announced to Cinco Fermentaciones that he would need to consult a travel agent about his return flight.

'I don't think that would be wise,' said his host.

Von Igelfeld raised an eyebrow. 'And why not?'

'Because Pedro expects you to stay,' said Cinco Fermentaciones. 'He telephoned me last night, after you had gone to bed. We are both to be in the Government.'

'That is quite unacceptable,' said von Igelfeld sharply. 'I have many other things to do.'

'It won't be for all that long,' said Cinco Fermentaciones. 'These governments don't last all that long. Eight, nine months perhaps. A year at the outside.'

'I still do not want to do it,' said von Igelfeld.

Cinco Fermentaciones sighed. 'In that case, I have no future.'

'I don't see what you mean,' said von Igelfeld. 'What's it got to do with your future?'

'If you're not in, then I'm not in,' said Cinco Fermentaciones. 'And if I'm not in the Government, then my enemies will kill me. By saying that you won't join, you're signing my death warrant. I shall have to make a will.'

Von Igelfeld was alarmed. 'But, please,' he said. 'I would not wish that to happen.' He paused. Perhaps he could serve in the Government for a short time and then resign. That might save Cinco Fermentaciones from his fate. He proposed this to Cinco Fermentaciones, who agreed that it would be a good compromise.

'Give it a month or so,' said Cinco Fermentaciones. 'Then you can resign. I'll be safely entrenched by then. Even better, I shall have myself appointed Ambassador to Paris or somewhere agreeable like that.'

Von Igelfeld agreed, reluctantly, of course, and his agreement cheered Cinco Fermentaciones, who had been looking rather despondent. Then, once they had finished their breakfast, they stepped out of the house into the large black limousine which Pedro had despatched to collect them. This took them through the streets of the Old Town to the Government Palace where Pedro, now wearing a handsome bottle-green uniform, very similar to the General's but distinguished by the addition of several extra gold stripes, met them on the steps.

That morning the Cabinet was sworn in and had its first

session. Von Igelfeld did not say much, but he noticed that many members seemed to defer to him on difficult points; and he nodded or shook his head, almost at random, but nonetheless with a firmness of purpose which seemed to impress his fellow Ministers. Then they adjourned for lunch, at which large quantities of the country's finest wines were served. The company at the table was congenial, and members of the Cabinet moved from chair to chair between courses, so that everybody could have the chance to talk to one another. It was after one of these changes that he found himself sitting next to Pedro.

'I can't tell you how grateful I am to you, Professor von Igelfeld,' he said. 'If it weren't for you, there might have been a terrible battle, which we might not have won.'

Von Igelfeld waved a hand in an airy fashion. 'It was really nothing,' he said. 'Just one shot.'

'One shot,' echoed Pedro. 'But one shot was enough to bring down a rotten government.'

'Well . . .'

'And because of that,' went on Pedro, 'I have decided that the right thing to do is to ask you to perform a special duty. It will not be too onerous, I hope, but it will be special.'

'I am at your service,' said von Igelfeld. Presumably this would be something to do with the Academy of Letters. Perhaps the General wanted to be proposed for membership now, or Pedro's cousin perhaps.

Pedro laid a hand on von Igelfeld's shoulder. 'I should like you – we would all like you to become President of the Republic.'

Von Igelfeld stared at him in complete astonishment. 'President?'

'Yes,' said Pedro. 'And I can see from your expression that you accept! Thank you! Thank you!'

Turning from von Igelfeld, Pedro jumped on to a chair, glass in hand. 'Fellow Ministers!' he shouted. 'Silence for a moment! I ask you now to rise to your feet and toast the new President of the Republic of Colombia, President Coronel Professor von Igelfeld! *Viva! Viva! Viva!*'

Von Igelfeld did not know what to do. He heard shouts of *Viva!* about his ears and his back was slapped by several enthusiastic Ministers. Then somebody slipped a broad red sash over his shoulder, and a band struck up somewhere in the background. He looked down at his plate. What time would it be in Germany now, he wondered? What time would it be out in the rational world?

The following two weeks were very tedious for von Igelfeld. Installed in the Presidential Palace, he had been given a comfortable office and a team of adjutants and secretaries. But there was really very little to do, apart from signing decrees, which were placed, ready-drafted in front of him on his desk. Occasionally people came to see him, but he found that they did not expect him to say anything, and so he merely sat there behind his desk and struggled with boredom and irritation while they spoke their piece. Occasionally he read the decrees that were placed before him, and once or twice he had to refuse to sign and sent them back to the officials with a stern note.

One such occasion was when a large elaborate document was placed before him and a pen put in his hand. He brushed aside the anxious official for a moment and began to read the text. As he did so, he became more and more alarmed.

'What is this?' he said at last. 'This document purports to be a declaration of war with Ecuador! What is the meaning of this?'

The official laughed nervously. 'It is not important, Señor Presidente. I suggest that you sign it. It is not important.'

'A declaration of war is not important?' snorted von Igelfeld. 'Is that what you're telling me?'

'Well, it's not a *serious* declaration of war,' said the official. 'Declarations of war don't mean quite the same thing in South America as they do elsewhere. They're more of a *statement*, really.'

'So this document does not create a state of war between us and Ecuador?' asked von Igelfeld. 'Is that what you're telling me?'

'Well, not exactly,' said the official unctuously. 'Technically we shall be at war with Ecuador, on the side of Peru. You may recall that they have had a long-standing dispute over the ownership of the Amazon Basin. Nothing really serious, of course, but they do go to war with one another every so often. If we join in, we will make a few incursions into Ecuador and perhaps blow up a few bridges. Not much more than that.'

'But,' said von Igelfeld, 'why on earth should we get involved in the first place? What's the point?'

The official smiled. '*El Presidente* will be aware of the fact that our air force is a little under strength. In fact, none of our planes works. Not one. Peru has offered us four new MIG fighters – four! – if we'll join them in a war against Ecuador. It's an absolute bargain.'

Von Igelfeld pursed his lips. 'I shall not countenance this,' he said crossly. 'Take this document away.'

The official nodded. He had not been too hopeful of getting the declaration of war approved, but it had still been worth a try. But he was angry, and he felt spiteful towards von Igelfeld.

'I shall have to ask the next President,' he said. 'He will be in office soon, I imagine.'

'Oh?' said von Igelfeld. 'When?'

'Two or three weeks,' said the official. 'After the *narcotraficantes* have disposed of Your Excellency.'

Von Igelfeld looked at the official. 'Disposed of me?'

The official looked sympathetic. 'Your Excellency is a brave man,' he said quietly. 'But then perhaps nobody has told Your Excellency why you were chosen for this office by Señor Pedro. He's the one who's running the country back there – Your Excellency is merely, how shall I put it delicately? – the figurehead. Señor Pedro knows that the *narcotraficantes* will assassinate whoever is President, and that's why they put Your Excellency in this position.' He paused, studying the effect of his words on von Igelfeld. 'I thought that Your Excellency would have known.'

'Of course I knew,' said von Igelfeld sharply. 'Any fool could work that out. Now please leave me alone. I have to telephone the German Ambassador to arrange to pay a State Visit next week.'

It was a very curious feeling arriving back in Germany as the President of Colombia. The German Ambassador had been most supportive, and had stressed to the German Foreign Ministry that the President did not wish to be greeted with excessive pomp, but nonetheless there were certain niceties to be observed and von Igelfeld was obliged to inspect a guard of honour and stand at attention for several minutes while the national anthems of the two countries were played. Then, after a brief talk with a German Minister, who seemed to be particularly interested in selling him a nuclear reactor, von Igelfeld insisted on being driven to the Institute. They had been notified, of course, and everybody was lining the steps when he arrived. They never did this when I was not a president, he thought bitterly, but that was human nature, he supposed.

Surrounded by his Colombian diplomatic officials and his aides-de-camp, von Igelfeld drank a cup of coffee in the coffee room with his old colleagues.

'My aunt will simply not believe this,' said the Librarian. 'I told her that you had become President of Colombia and she became slightly confused, I'm sorry to say. In fact, the doctor was a little bit cross with me for telling her this as he said that she should not be subjected to excessive excitement.'

'Yes, yes,' said von Igelfeld. 'That is very true.' But he sounded as if his mind was not on the Librarian's tale, and indeed it was not. He had made his decision, and now he would implement it. The moment had come.

'I wish to make a speech,' said von Igelfeld to his Colombian staff. 'Make sure that somebody writes down what I have to say.'

'Certainly, Señor Presidente,' said his private secretary. 'We shall do as you order.'

'Good,' said von Igelfeld, clearing his throat. 'Dear colleagues, dear civil servants, diplomats, colonels, military attachés et cetera et cetera. In recognition of the close ties of friendship between the Republic of Germany and the Republic of Colombia, it is my pleasure today to invest our dear German hosts with well-deserved honours of the Colombian state.'

'Professor Florianus Prinzel, I hereby confer on you the Order of the Andes, First Class. This is in recognition of your contribution to scholarship, and its first-class nature.'

Prinzel smiled, and bowed to von Igelfeld, who nodded in acknowledgement and then continued: 'And on the Librarian, Herr Huber, I have great pleasure in conferring the title of Honorary Corresponding Librarian of the Colombian Academy of Letters.'

Herr Huber was too overcome to do anything, but his gratitude was palpable, and so von Igelfeld proceeded to the third task.

'And now, on Professor Detlev Amadeus Unterholzer, in recognition of his contribution to scholarship, I now confer the Order of the Andes . . . ' There was a moment of complete silence, a moment in which von Igelfeld confronted one of the greatest temptations of his moral life, far greater than any quandary which had confronted him in the heat of the Colombian revolution. It would have been easy, oh so easy, to say, *Third Class*, as the Belgians had said to him. That would have taught Unterholzer. That would have paid him back for using his room without his permission; but no, he said instead, with a flourish, *First Class*, and Unterholzer, weak with emotion, stepped forward and took his hand and shook it.

All that remained for von Igelfeld to do was to resign as President of Colombia, which he did immediately after carrying out these last generous acts of liberality. His resignation speech was short, and dignified.

'I have served Colombia to the best of my ability,' he said, 'but now the torch must be handed to another. I therefore appoint dear Señor Pedro as my successor, with all the powers and privileges of the office. May he discharge the duties in an honest and decent way, remembering that in a bad country – and, please, I am not for a moment suggesting that Colombia is a bad country – there are many ordinary people who will be counting on those in high office to remember their suffering and their aspirations. My place is here. This is where I have been called to serve. *Viva el Presidente Pedro! Viva la Patria!*'

And with that he sat down. There was, of course, a certain amount of confusion amongst the Colombian officials, but they soon recovered their composure and went off to lunch in a restaurant

which Herr Huber was able to recommend to them. Then von Igelfeld went to his room and began to attend to his mail. There was so much to read, and he would be busy writing letters all that afternoon and well into the following day.

He looked about him. Were there signs of Unterholzer having been in his room? He thought that some of the books had been moved, although he could not be sure. He stopped himself. He remembered being at a window, looking down an avenue of trees, and waiting for an army to advance. He remembered Dolores Quinta Barranquilla standing beneath the rising helicopter and waving to them as the blades of the aircraft cut into the thin Andean air. And he heard again the cries of *Viva!* and the expression of sheer relief on the faces of the guerrillas and the soldiers as they realised that nobody was going to ask them to die after all. And he realised then that there were more important things to worry about, and that we must love those with whom we live and work, and love them for all their failings, manifest and manifold though they be.